THE PASSIONATE ATTENTION OF AN INTERESTING MAN

A Novella and Four Stories

Ethan Mordden

Magnus Books, an imprint of Riverdale Avenue Books
5676 Riverdale Ave. Suite 101
New York, NY 10471

Library of Congress Cataloging-In-Publication Data available. Printed in the United States of America on acid-free paper.

First Edition
ISBN: 978-1-936833-22-1

Edited by: Don Weise
Cover by: Linda Kosarin, The Art Department
Cover photo by: Rob Lang/ RobLangImages.com
Interior layout by www.formatting4U.com
www.magnusbooks.com

Praise for Ethan Mordden

"A deliberately funny book, laced with laughs and irony, that sometimes makes one cry…ingenious and sophisticated."

—*The Los Angeles Times* on *I've a Feeling We're Not in Kansas Anymore*

"Mordden explores a tricky moral universe in which emotional loyalty is exalted but sexual fidelity is not assumed… There is a real sense of pain amid the zingers."

—*The New York Times* on *Some Men Are Lookers*

"Ethan Mordden is a master craftsman. His style combines the satirical urbanity of Juvenal, the wit of Oscar Wilde, the intelligence and drawing-room sophistication of Jane Austen."

—*Bay Windows* on *Everybody Loves You*

"Combining literary wit with vivid characters…his vigorous prose could be as easily compared to parts of *Ulysses* as to Wilde's aphorisms."

—*Publishers Weekly* (starred review) on *Some Men Are Lookers*

"Epic, lively, entertaining…Mordden's big book full of feeling and humor is going to keep a lot of readers happy."

—*Washington Post Book World* on *How Long Has This been Going On?*

Table of Contents

Tom	1
Hopelessly Devoted to You	89
The Flippety Flop	125
The Suite	141
The Food of Love	185
Acknowledgments	225
About the Author	227

TOM

The Passionate Attention of an Interesting Man

Lloyd's first piece for the paper discussed the "gourmet" salad bar in the food shop in the new mall. Or, more precisely, what Lloyd discussed was the behavior of its customers as they interacted with the platters of chicken fingers and tortellini and each other. Lloyd's second piece toured the remodeling of the gym two doors down from the food shop and his third the gym's grand opening and how the genders inspected each other. He entitled it "Cruising."

Then came Lloyd's fourth piece, on the town's spoiled rich kids—*really* rich, the heirs and heiresses who seemed to know each other and no one else. Lloyd wrote of their lingo, attitudes, and rituals as if they were his, too. Instantly, Lloyd became a man of local note, recognized and invited. More important, the reading of his column, *What State Am I In*? went to the top of everybody's daily activity sheet. Lloyd had to turn his report on rich kids into a series, and he found himself with something rare in the life of a freelance writer: job security.

Lloyd's editor found Lloyd's topics perplexing nonetheless. Gyms are something you belong to, not something you read about.

"They're all alike," the editor said. "Bicycles and yoga classes, no?"

"The *gyms* are alike," Lloyd told him. "The clientele varies. When they're keyed up and playful, they put a place into spin."

Lloyd's ease in the tossing of language made him not only the journalist of the moment but agreeably provincial: a booster of local endeavors. Folks enjoyed hearing that the food shop in their mall rivaled those in your conceited eastern metropolises, or that their gym could pass in California. Lloyd knew how to flatter while maintaining high standards, which was both friendly and impressive of him, and, as his editor had to admit, Lloyd knew How To Be Where. It was while hanging out in Avatar that he got the idea for the series he called "Bon Ton Brats." And, thanks to Lloyd, Avatar became, overnight, the trendiest bar in town.

At thirty-six, Lloyd was a bit senior for the ambiance; rumor held that no one over a certain age could get in at all. But Lloyd was handsome and fit, and he had a great smile, with the teeth of a Steinway. Anyway, on Lloyd thirty-six played as twenty-nine: because he dressed young and slanged young. In fact, his first column on the culture of gilded youth treated almost nothing but their lingo, which Lloyd spoke with the deadpan flair of a native. To tire of something was *to spat with it*, as in "I have *so* spat with Lady Antebellum." To get rid of someone—especially a boy or girl friend—was *to toast* him or her. This could be expanded to the outside world, as in "voters toasted the incumbent on election day." Even if—as Lloyd noted in his column—"There is very little outside world in these kids' lives."

On rare occasions, something, somehow, impinged upon their liberty, as when a disapproving parent grounded them. This was known as *going dark*. Yet in fact there were no parents to speak of in the world of the bon ton brat, it seemed. They were rich kids so densely spoiled that one could more exactly think of them as autonomous twenty-two-year-olds with unmaxable plastic and the civic spirit of a motorcycle gang. It was summer, so they were on vacation: from what? The particular group that Lloyd met in Avatar—the kids on whom he based his articles—had just been graduated from college, yet they appeared to entertain no career plans. The boys looked forward to inheriting fortunes and the girls to spending them. Portia was engaged (or promised, or something) to Clark, for instance. Yet they didn't act like fiancés. She was too busy stealing kisses from her best friend, Annamarie. And Clark flirted obsessively with *his* best friend, Junior.

It was Portia who first brought Lloyd into this circle, approaching him in Avatar with a boldness that told Lloyd—as he reported to his readers—that the traditional usages of gender behavior were over. Portia was on her way back to her friends from the ladies' room when, passing Lloyd, she slowed, smiled, and then stopped to ask him, "Now, what is such an impressive piece of merchandise doing all alone in a social club? If I may ask, my dear sir."

Lloyd had scarcely started speaking when Portia

took his hand and gently pulled him along to meet her friends. She was extremely pretty, beautifully made in all particulars with light auburn hair. *Very* light, Lloyd thought, in that incredibly appealing silky wonder that no man fails to respond to. And she wasn't really forward, just…game. *Ready*, you might say. A charmingly independent young woman. Lloyd was used to scoring, but guys usually had to work for it, had to listen and invent, setting off firecrackers of poetry and courtship.

Not here. Portia and her crew didn't waste time on preludes. Once among them, Lloyd found that he was the one being scored. Portia and Annamarie and Clark and Junior were confident and curious and they moved in on you quickly. They loved that Lloyd was a writer, that he was with the paper, that he would quote them. "Set me down in your paragraphs," Portia promised, "and I'll fuck you crippled."

She said this sweetly, even innocently; girls were so different nowadays. Lloyd could get a column or two out of *that*, he thought, looking around Avatar at its new American version of Bright Young Things grouping, dissolving, regrouping. Grandstanding and confiding. Exploiting youth and looks as the tools of performance art. Some worked in modes so new they had yet to be described while others were as square as a malted with two straws, sweethearts sipping to some retro tune. Yes, the "Theme from *A Summer Place*." Dancing the stroll and wearing each other's clothing, his tie and her scarf. But four of these kids—Lloyd's four—were style setters and clearly in the core clique.

It turned out that they had known one another from preschool playdates on and were as egosyntonic as a commedia dell'arte troupe. Was it rehearsed when Portia and Annamarie put their heads together, literally, to say the same thing in the same words at the same time while Clark leaned in to attend and Junior caressed the back of Clark's neck?

So they were showoffs, ideal for Lloyd's agenda: good copy. They'd photograph well, too, both of the girls really quite fetching and the boys muscled pups. Pulling out his pad and pen, Lloyd took dictation as the kids posed and quoted away. They told Lloyd of intricate rituals in the maintenance of status, of diplomacy with grownups, of recognizing one's peers and discouraging moochers.

Anthropology.

"Does that pad come with spell check?" Clark asked Lloyd.

"How old are you?" said Annamarie. "Emotionally."

"Who's prettier," Junior wanted to know, "Clark or me?"

"But how much money is there in journalism?" Portia asked. "They tell of fortunes paid for celebrity gossip. Could you be tattler to the stars?"

Lloyd said, "Newcomer in town takes notes on definitive local youngsters, only to discover that he finds them too charming to exploit."

Junior preened as Clark asked, "What is that—the talking you just did? Is it Hollywood?"

Lloyd nodded. "It's called a 'log line.'"

"Is that how they pitch a new idea?"

"No," Lloyd answered. "The pitch markets the ware. The log line analyzes it. Here...The *Wizard of Oz*. A heroine enjoys marvelous adventures, only to discover that all she really needs is a home filled with love."

"Now me," said Clark—but Junior cut in with "*Clark: The Movie*. A hero thinks he's the most winning specimen on the planet, but most girls find him—"

"You have to use 'only to discover,'" Lloyd explained, as Clark aimed a warning finger at Junior. "The log line states an irony, and 'only to discover' is the listener's warning ramp."

Portia said, "My parents plan a wedding so white it must be held during a blizzard, only to discover that I've had carnal knowledge of every hottie in town. The eligible ones, of course. Exclusively."

"Everyone except Junior," Clark added.

Here Portia and Junior exchanged the briefest of glances. But Clark caught them.

"What?" he cried, turning accusingly on Junior, who held his ground, half-smiling. "You two *when*? You *where*? Do I have to set detectives on you?"

"I had Junior first," Annamarie told Lloyd, nodding at his pad. "Write it down, mister."

"My goodness," said Lloyd, in *faux*-naïve, stretching out the vowels so they'd know he was jesting. "The conspiracies around here."

"You'll have to come to the next pool party," Portia told Lloyd. "A sophisticate *so* raises the tone."

She took Lloyd's hand in hers, massaging the separations between the fingers.

"I love a sophisticated man," she explained.

"Whoa, there," said Clark. "Because he's older? I'll be sophisticated, too, at that age."

No one knew Lloyd's age, or anything else about him, because he was an orphan. A foundling in fact. He seldom brought it up, because it made nice people feel awkward and devious people wary, as if being an orphan was a con, a setup before you hit them for a loan. Lloyd himself was an opportunist, but an open one, too breezy of style to trouble to connive. Early on, he took a wife because she ran a very profitable business manufacturing children's clothes, and she accepted Lloyd because he was broke but entertaining. She agreed to support him while he assembled credits in the "looks" professions—as actor, television personality, model. He did some local work, hosted idiotic events (there was actually a Miss Steak contest), and wrote. Then his wife's brother suddenly turned up.

She had never mentioned him before, and Lloyd asked her why.

"Oh, Jack is so…you know" is all she said.

She could have said a lot more, for Jack was a questionable item. He conversed exclusively in conspiracy theory—not just who killed the Kennedys but who was protecting the interplanetary alien population. Worse, he clonked in and out of the house throughout the night on unnamed errands. Finally, Lloyd came home unexpectedly to hear his wife and Jack making jubilant love.

Lloyd packed and fled; he never heard from or about his wife again. Broke and entertaining once more, Lloyd oddjobbed around, trying to put his intelligence to work as a fulltime writer. It's an easy life, at least, once you catch on with a readership. But Lloyd found it hard to break in. He kept moving and starting up again, as one sometimes has to. He wore a moustache for a time, but it ages you. He tried dating rich gay men, but the sex was irritating.

And now, in the latest new town, Lloyd had finally found work that matched his skills: as movie critic, copyeditor, and, mainly, features writer for the daily. He was not only prominent but solvent—and, as long as he didn't have to run a car, the salary floated him. He was hunting for a place to live within a bike ride of everywhere he needed to go, including the North Side, where the rich kids held their recurring pool parties in Portia's family's house. It was an indoor pool, a big one, heated in winter, because the doctor told Portia's father that he had a choice: swim laps each day, every day of the year, or die quite soon.

Portia's father was wealthy enough to tear off a wing of his home and erect a vast pool house in its place. Folks said, "Golly!" and he just shrugged. There were swimming pools at Junior's and Annamarie's, but these were backyard affairs. Just as Mrs. Astor's ballroom of the four hundred made her the sovereign of New York society all those chronicles ago, "Portia's pool" gave Portia an uncontested social regime. She ruled with a light touch. It was the boys, Lloyd suspected, who decreed who was to be included and who left out. They called it *uninstalling*. The pool parties busied these kids two or three nights a week, and there was always a guest list. One dropped in at peril of hostile rebuff, especially from Clark.

"Let's uninstall Hardin Wensley for a bit," Clark would say. "I'm cooling on him."

"Yes!" Junior would agree. Then he'd say, "Why?" Junior loved to stand with Clark when he wasn't standing against him.

"Why?" Annamarie echoed.

Clark replied, "He's so corny is why."

"He's corny," Junior told Annamarie, as if translating from a foreign tongue.

There were servants at Portia's pool parties, but no chaperones, much less parents—no grownups with authority. Portia's father had laid down strict rules, all the same, such as a ban on cell phones. He said they made kids stupid, encouraging them to talk when they had nothing to say. Besides, important people don't answer ringing phones. They are given messages, some of which they do not respond to.

Lloyd and his readers found every tidbit of the story interesting, with its blend of youth and money. Yet these kids had no content in any real sense; they offered a kind of pointlessly meaningful lesson in how to make the most of endless summer leisure. If they were special at all, it was for the stylish way in which they wasted time. After an hour of splashing around in the water, Clark would climb out and ooze his way around the pool like a stripper. Junior, acolyte and rival, would perform his robot dance. Then it was time for a pizza snack: cook would appear, and Portia would order by describing her mood. "Up too late and seen it all," she would say. "Needing to be soothed." Cook would nod and make—from scratch—paper-thin slices with mushroom and basil. Or Portia would say, "Adventurous," and the gang would get the works. Do you, too, want to live like this? was the question that Lloyd's columns seemed to ask his readers. Would you happy in Portia's world?

Would Lloyd?

And here's an arresting surprise: these all but unsupervised young people had no contact with drugs of pleasure or with those who did. Names would come up: of kids who got into coke and stole from their friends and weren't allowed at Portia's any more. Clark would run a finger across his throat, and Junior would cry, "It was bound to happen!" as though drugging, thievery, and social ruin were sins that came as a set.

In fact, these kids had a puritanical streak about almost every indulgence except sex. Lloyd discovered this at his very first pool party, when he entered the bathroom to find Junior's swimsuit around his ankles and Portia sucking his cock. Backing out as suavely as possible, Lloyd brushed against Annamarie, who gently pushed him back into the room with a pianissimo "Am I late for the contest?" Then she pulled Lloyd's Speedos down to make a twin with Portia.

It was Lloyd's theory that most women sucked you off as incompetently as possible in the hope that you would never ask for a repeat. In sex—according to Lloyd—women liked one act only: having a marriage license. They seemed not to enjoy sex but rather to tolerate it in trade for certain privileges, such as childbirth and knowing the exact location of their husband second by second.

Portia and Annamarie, then, were rare women, avid for sex and extremely good at it. In the progressive—or simply absentee—atmosphere that Portia's parents created, there might be strictures about cell phones but not, apparently, about physical contact. Yet how fastidiously Annamarie slipped a non-lubricated condom onto Lloyd's member—from where? he wondered—before she began. These kids had all the flaws of youth except recklessness. They really were golden: healthy and handsome and free of danger.

And now Lloyd was giving them the fame of the county in his columns even as readers pestered the paper for more. E-mail commentary tripled, subscriptions jumped, professional loudmouths hectored the subject from pulpit and cable talk-show set. Lloyd himself began to entertain a crazy dream: either of the two girls—but preferably the auburn Portia—would fall for Lloyd, marry him, and save him from the vexatious day-to-day of slogging through life on the material expectations of an orphan.

Lloyd knew it was crazy. Girls of Portia's status didn't marry men of unknown origin. Lloyd couldn't even say whether or not he was single: he had escaped but never actually dissolved his early marriage.

Yet Portia—and Annamarie, and a few of the others of their coterie—unmistakably found Lloyd attractive. He knew how that worked. Anyway, by the standards of the region Lloyd was a hotshot, so full of ideas and observations that he charmed almost everyone. He was careful to do this in a soft way, in order not to alarm or provoke. He never got into politics or religion—so often the same thing these days. And he never risked looking like a showboater. When Portia and Annamarie held one of their blowjob contests and, after sampling the contestants, declared Lloyd the winner, he never preened but rather let his features go blank, an ideal way to receive Clark's "Fierce, bro!"

And Lloyd knew how to avoid being drawn into the kids' favorite sport, bickering. When Portia would prefer Lloyd to Clark on some pretext—as Portia loved to do—Lloyd would contrive to look skinny and futile, no man's rival. Indeed, Lloyd would look on uninvolved as Portia and Clark merrily bayed at each other, to the play-by-play critique and footnoting of Annamarie and Junior. This would usually break out at about eleven-thirty of an evening, after the rest of the crowd had departed and Lloyd was alone with the central quartet.

"Really, Clark," goes Portia. "With your squalid blandishments and historically suspect family oil revenues!"

"What suspect?" Clark will ask.

Portia quotes: "'Behind every great fortune lies a great crime.'"

"Look who's talking! Miss Oil Money of the Year!"

"Portia is way collegiate, Clark" comes from Annamarie, though you could never tell whether she was serious or riffing. "She commands fantastic wisdom, and—no! You cut out that silly swimsuit dance! Junior, make Clark stop!"

"Stop, Clark," says Junior, looking as if he'd like to fall into Clark's arms. After a moment, as Clark does not stop, Junior joins him, trying to imitate Clark's moves.

"These hopeless local beaux," Portia remarks.

"What do you expect," Annamarie laments, "when you invite the neighborhood?"

"At least we can count on our suave cosmo role-model," says Portia, beaming at Lloyd.

Dancing past them, Clark says, "I'm suave for my years."

"You?" cries Portia. "You're rough as nails!"

"I'm suave, too," Junior puts in.

"I have the edge," says Clark, "because I'm a love entrepreneur." He stops dancing, and Junior stops, too.

Fetching his pad and pen, Lloyd asks Clark if he can quote him in a column.

"It was bound to happen!" Junior cries.

"Quote me?" Clark replies to Lloyd. "I love that concept, dude."

It was Lloyd's self-defensive flattery, a way of pacifying the anger of strangers before they got angry: tell them they sound interesting.

The advertisement, in Lloyd's own paper, was brusque and concise:

Housemate wanted.
Own bedroom, bath.
Landlord on premises. Rules apply.
Smokers no way.
Rent is low if I like you.

The address was attractive, across the road from the very mall that Lloyd had started his columns on, with the salad bar and the refurbished gym. The area was fifteen minutes from Portia's by bicycle, an older part of town that was half middle-class domestic and half parvenu slick: old two-storeys with cluttered garages surprised by apartment complexes and trendy leisure shops.

The landlord, on the phone, spoke with the voice of his ad, tough and plain and maybe a bit old-fashioned, as befits a guy who places his messages in newsprint instead of on Craigslist. Lloyd arranged to look at the room in three days, on the following Saturday, but first he decided to bike over to scout the quartier.

It was a perfect fit. The house in question looked trim and happy: a ranch-style with what appeared to be an extension built for extra bedrooms when the kids arrived, perhaps some time in the late 1980s. Revisiting the mall across the way, Lloyd noted with pleasure a laundry, a Starbucks, a vast grocery outlet, and a pharmacy (all very handy when you're going carless) along with the gym and food shop. Lloyd took an early lunch there, before it got too jammed, and once again he was amused at the etiquette of the buffet, as the veteran gourmets swooped down on their platters of fashion while newbies stared at a bill of fare too dense for their modest sense of free will. Lloyd watched them study how the other diners did it, and "I'll Have What They're Having" became his next piece, this one made of interviews with the customers. Pedalling home with his notes, Lloyd outlined, wrote, and clicked the column off to his editor for a next-day printing. Twenty-four hours later, the eatery tripled its business.

Then came Saturday, the day of Lloyd's appointment with the house guy. Lloyd biked over early so he'd have time to get off the wheels, sweat out the exertion, handkerchief himself dry, and look good for the landlord. A big blond high-schooler pulled the door open, inspecting Lloyd and offering a handshake that smarted for minutes. Then he beckoned Lloyd inside with a blunt gesture.

He was not a teenager, it turned out, but the landlord himself, twenty-something and massive, the muscles of his upper torso aggressive in a white T over light-blue jeans and yellow Timberlands. How does the Danish lookout phrase it in *Beowulf*? "Never before have I beheld a greater warrior on earth." He wasn't much of a talker, though. He asked questions about Lloyd's work and finances, but he kept his opinions to himself.

He didn't offer much biography, either. Nor did he say what line of work he was in, although, young as he was, he did own the home outright, having inherited it from his father. And he admitted this much: his dad had held down a respectable job and raised four kids by himself. "Because life isn't fair," the young man explained, "and my mom died young."

And then, towering over Lloyd, he went right into what he asked of a housemate and how he viewed the world, "because there are too many freaks and swindlers who never get punished for their crimes." Then there was a pause. Lloyd filled it in with "You're awfully young to own, though. A house, I mean."

That created another pause. In fact, the young man was twenty-four, though he didn't say so at the time. He didn't say anything apropos at the time: he was always saying something else or nothing at all. For instance, after another pause, he suddenly told Lloyd that he lived alone and took everything very seriously. It seemed like a line from another scene, even another play. Then he said that he had unbreakable rules that he might as well get into right the way off. 'Cause there are rules to live by, so he believed. And if anyone says he's wrong, well, he may just have to get rough about it.

His name, he said, was Tom Buckner. "You should know by now," he added, almost as if challenging Lloyd.

Who simply responded by giving his own name, then suffering another crushing handshake.

Tom Buckner's house rules were fine with Lloyd, and the house itself was wonderful. The people who had lived in it, Tom's people, had clearly loved it, kept it working well and looking right—fresh paint, sturdy old furniture, and a faint smell of cleansing pine. The room and bath on offer, reached down a far hall from the day rooms, looked very comfortable. There was even a kitchenette along one wall of the bedroom, with a tiny refrigerator and a toaster oven. Yogurts and toast, Lloyd thought—his favorite midnight snack.

But here's an odd moment, as the two men walked by the only door in the house that was closed. Lloyd kept on moving, but Tom dallied. It was momentary, like slowing for a speed bump. Nevertheless, Lloyd felt a silent roar of energy in the way Tom said, in these words alone, "My daddy's room."

Lloyd thought he might have got Tom's very limited biography wrong. "He still lives here?"

"He died."

Before Lloyd could rejoin with the customary regrets, Tom took Lloyd's arm with the authority of a drill sergeant and steered Lloyd away down the hall with "Show you the garage."

They traveled through the kitchen to a back door, into an index of middle-class life: tires, storm windows, toys, ages of man. You could almost hear children's joyous cries, reclaiming hobbycrafts or hefting shovels to clear away snow.

"So full of stuff now," said Tom, "that I use the carport, and I couldn't tell you where another vehicle would go. You drive?"

"I run a bike."

Tom grunted pleasantly.

Gazing around the garage, Lloyd said, "You have sisters."

"How would you know that, now?"

"I see two bake ovens. Two art kits."

"You got it right, anyway."

Taking hold of one of the drawing sets, Lloyd asked, "May I?"

Tom nodded.

"This was well used," Lloyd observed as he opened it. "The pieces have seen a lot of work, yet they're all neatly in place, waiting for..." Lloyd smiled. Gently pulling out a stub of chalk, he added, "Someone was very fond of carmine."

Tom had moved off a bit, evidently with some purpose.

"My daddy encouraged my sisters to be artistic," he said, absently. Then, with more intention: "My brother and I would build things. Dad taught us right here."

He indicated an elaborate tool bay extending behind an old refrigerator and not easily admired till Lloyd walked over to Tom.

The bay was virtually a place of its own, resting in a kind of military formation: a broad worktable, three stools evenly spaced in front of it, a sawhorse, and an astonishing array of software, fanatic and beautiful in their order, their symmetry.

"He showed us here, my dad. My brother and me."

"Do you still use it?"

"No."

Tom picked up the sole freestanding piece on the worktable surface, a miniature locomotive and tender sitting on a small section of mounted track. They looked absurdly small in Tom's monster grasp, and Lloyd felt a pointless twinge of irritation. Yes, all right, you're a handsome guy, but why do you have to be so darn big about it?

But what Lloyd said, guided by the "G. E. R." on the tender's side, was "That's a Great Eastern, isn't it? Did you make it from a kit?"

Startled, Tom looked quizzically at Lloyd, then silently handed him the model.

Rather than chance dropping it, Lloyd set it on the worktable, saying, "Ours all came ready-made. Some modelers build their own, though. Amazing, isn't it?" Lloyd was smiling, affable, sound housemate material. He'd be neat and unobtrusive; you could just tell. "They assemble all those parts and literally fashion their own trains."

Tom pushed the little model closer to Lloyd: an unreadable but perhaps friendly gesture.

"Did you run a railroad when you were a kid?" Lloyd asked.

"We wanted to. But my dad said it was wasteful.

All that work to build it, and then what do you get? A lot of choo-choo, my dad said. He liked us making things we could use." Then: "You can hold it," Tom urged Lloyd.

After a moment's hesitation, Lloyd picked it up, and Tom asked, "What kind of railroad did you run? Did you lay it out yourself?"

"It was given to us, actually. The whole thing, with a mountain and a tunnel and a town. Märklin HO gauge. A beautiful set, though it didn't have a trainyard. We had to pick out the cars from a box and plop them onto the lines."

He raised the locomotive and its coal car in the air, holding it between them as if in illustration of something.

"You favor a roundhouse, then?" Tom asked him. "You like the reality of it?"

"Well, but it takes up too much room, I suppose." Lloyd set the train model back on the worktable. "If I could build my own layout, I'd have to find some original solution."

"Tell me what you do again, Lloyd."

Lloyd told him, and Tom suggested they talk business over coffee. But when Tom led Lloyd to the kitchen and got out the instant, Lloyd suggested they take the conversation to the Starbucks across the road.

"Rich people's coffee," said Tom.

"We'll order their coffee of the day. That's for the proles."

"What's that word?"

"Regular folks. My treat?"

At the coffee bar, Lloyd ran the chat: because otherwise they would have seemed to be meditating, adrift in the silences of Tom. Or Tom would blurt out something way off-topic.

"They're looking at you," he suddenly told Lloyd.

"Who?"

"Chicks. My view, nine o'clock and two-thirty. Go ahead and turn, check them out. They like it."

Instead, Lloyd took a sip of coffee and said, "You don't suppose maybe they're wondering about the big Viking sitting across from me?"

Tom took another look at the girls. "One of them's waving," he said, waving back.

"Think of all the advantages," Lloyd went on, "that a man can have—looks, money, intelligence. He could be famous as a local dignitary, or even a rock star of some sort. Or competing on a reality show—famous at the Olive Garden. But say a guy is good-looking and also really big-sized, like you. *Everyone* responds to that, because it's what any man wants to be and what any woman wants to hook up with. Everywhere you go, you're tilting the room."

Tom grinned. "You practicing for more newspaper writings?"

He helped himself to another pause, and now Lloyd was starting to enjoy them.

"This coffee's nice," Tom finally said. "It's deep and crazy. Rich roast."

"Is one of them cute, at least?" Lloyd asked. "The chicks?"

"They're all right."

"Skip it, then."

Lloyd tried a smile. He had three; this was the

emptily engaging one. It was known to charm, but Tom just looked at it.

"Say more about your model layout," Tom said. "How did it come to you all made?"

"A Quaker family did that thing they sometimes do, when the kids have had enough joy of something and now it has to be shared with the less fortunate. And…brace yourself for the fun part…I'm an orphan."

Tom thought that over. "Like from the orphanage?"

Lloyd nodded. "See, that's who Quakers give their toys away to. One day, out of nowhere, it just arrived, and—"

"I'm sorry for your misfortune."

"No, I'm fine with it. Really. We all start somewhere."

"It's supposed to start with a family."

"Well…yes. But the sisters were very nice to us, and Father James gave us the…moral fiber thing. St. Catherine's, this was." Pensively swirling his coffee as if he had said all he ought to, Lloyd suddenly continued with "I kind of liked it, actually. Except when they farmed us out to foster homes. They had to, because of, like, *no* budget. Still, we'd wind up with the worst people. We always ran away, even the girls. Fifty, sixty miles sometimes. Father James would try to be grim about it, but he was secretly glad to see us back."

Now it was Lloyd who commanded the pause. Then, as if coming out of a trance, he said, "Oh! Sorry. We were theming trains, weren't we?"

"No, what did they do to you in those foster homes?" Tom asked. "'Cause my daddy was strict with us, but he never—"

"They weren't strict, fosters, they just hated us. They took kids in for the state money, is what."

"Man, that's hard on children."

"It toughened us up, I suppose. It taught us to create our own lives."

What a liar. Lloyd is fragile and has been dependent on the good will of stronger beings as long as he can remember. Lloyd's a courtier, an actor.

"My daddy was too severe with my sisters, I always felt," said Tom. "Girls being of tender disposition. But he was one of your cold-hearted types in general. Efficient about everything. It came with his line of work."

"What did he do?"

"What I mean, he wasn't demonstrative." Taking a swig of his coffee (inundated at the accessories desk with half and half), Tom put in, "Now, I sure do like this coffee. How come I didn't know about this place?"

Pausing yet again, for what appeared to be an appraising look at Lloyd, Tom decided to go on: "Dad was a loving guy, all the same. He struggled to give us as much as he could afford, and never once did he duck out when we needed him. You will read nowadays on the net about a dude my very age, old enough to vote and marry, and he's into his credit card for a party in a strip club. 'Cause he got through college. And the bill was fifty thousand dollars."

After another gulp of coffee, Tom nodded. "Yes, sir. Fifty whole thousand jokers. His daddy's protesting the bill, of course. But what for does that kid need a strip club to celebrate college? What kind of education did he get, to end when a slut licks your ear while your buddies make yipping noises? For fifty thousand dollars, you should be scoring Anne Hathaway! What'd *he* get? Cherry Jubilee or some such! Fifty thousand—you ever make that in a *year*? F'I were his daddy, I would surely punish him for his crimes. But some of these modern parents…all shout and no *do*."

Two couples walked by their table on the way out, and one girl, in a halter top with a tempting bare midriff, gave Tom a lingering eye-fuck. Both men saw it, and with some this can provoke an ego-war sequence. But Tom simply turned back to Lloyd with "I've already got a date, name of Lucy. How's two hundred a month sound?"

"For…Oh, the room." Now Lloyd paused, just for effect. "In fact—"

"Okay. Make it a hundred."

Lloyd's stunned hesitation. Then: "I'll take it, Tom."

Lloyd's first weeks as Tom's housemate were uneventful in an almost solitary way, as Tom spent most of his weekend with Lucy and was out each weekday on his day job, topping this with a two-hour gym addiction. By the time he got home with his brown bag of a dinner—a sandwich or some diner's tired old Special of the Day—Lloyd would often have gone off to socialize with "the Portias" or whatever other merry group he was cultivating. Lloyd is socially nimble and on the make.

Tom's house rules were entirely about security.

No friends over at any time, no giving out of the address over the internet—"Smart guys get a P. O. box," said Tom—and a strict curfew of twelve o'clock midnight. As Tom explained it, he didn't want to come out of a heavy sleep at all hours not knowing why he was hearing noises in his house.

"And you don't need to be stirring," said Tom. "You have your own fridge and bathroom, and if you lean to be night-thirsty you can set up a water jug and glass in your room, like me. Preparation. Control. And you should know that I don't like a rebellious housemate."

"I won't be rebellious, Tom."

When they did cross paths, they were companionable enough, and Tom might bring forth one of his books on model railroading and initiate a discussion. Store-bought models or make-your-owns? Weathered facades on the buildings or clean-cut? How many trains to operate? Wiring, geographing, backgrounds, kit-bashing. Tom said he would love to see shots of Lloyd's old layout, but Lloyd had no photographs of anything. He wasn't maintaining his past: he was in flight from it.

The two men made it a regular thing to meet on Saturday mornings over coffee, though Lloyd had to persuade Tom to acquire a grinder so he could brew them both the true-bean drink. And Tom declared that donuts dunked into real coffee tasted twice as good.

"You never argue with me," said Tom on one of these Saturdays. "Everybody else? Non-stop bullshit all the time. Resist me whenever I need something, always some damnhell reason made of nothing. You just say yes. Like I have a new idea about the mail, 'cause I never know whether I'm seeing it all if you bring it in. So how about from now on just leave it in the mailbox and let me pick it up?"

"Okay," said Lloyd.

"See?"

"I just don't like fighting," Lloyd explained. "Most guys are waging permanent ego war, you know. They press for control. '*Give me, give me*.' And if you dare thwart their will about anything, they turn on you as if you were the enemy."

"They will be punished for their crimes," said Tom mildly, as he poured more milk into his coffee. He cultivated a set of key phrases, tirelessly quoting them. "Rebellious" was anyone who blocked his agenda. "Obedient" was high praise. Consideration of others was the rule to live by, and "punishment for their crimes" befell those who broke the rule.

Every serious relationship reaches a tipping point, when it slips from light over into dense: from "friends" to *friends*. For instance: hot day, need water, buddy exits the store with a single large bottle for you to share. It's a marker. The subject is trust, and trust is everything.

Or this: Tom comes home one evening with a to-go dinner just as Lloyd is sitting down to fish sticks and spaghetti. Tom had scarcely lunched and then got caught up in overtime, and he is now back from the gym ravening like a lion. Stuck with cold anything in a brown bag, Tom gazes upon Lloyd's old-fashioned hot homemade with the look of one who has somehow managed to hurt his own feelings.

Lloyd, about to squeeze lemon onto the fish, asked, "Do you want my dinner, Tom? I can make myself another in a jiffy."

Tom knew he should express gratitude and say no. But he was madly hungry and Lloyd's meal looked irresistible, set out in a curved-bottom wooden bowl with the fish nested beside the pasta in a delicate red-and-yellow sauce.

"Take it," said Lloyd, as he happily pushed the bowl across the table, then went into the kitchen. It's a marker.

Tom immediately dug in, calling out, "Could I have seconds while you're at it?"

So Lloyd made two more servings, and when he gave Tom his second plate (and a hunk of Italian bread), Tom gobbled it up as he had the first.

"You were hungry," Lloyd observed.

"That's a tasty recipe," Tom replied as he scarfed up the last of the sauce with the bread. "After my work and the gym, I don't always get a square meal."

"Tom, you never get a square meal. You're going to fast-food your way through life."

"Time," Tom explained. "Convenience." Then: "You eat slow, the way kids do."

"Would you like me to make you dinner now and again? Cooking for two is as easy as—"

"Yes, I want that, and why is this sauce so nice?"

"It's my own invention, where you…Tom, why do you always eat take-out and donuts?"

"Sometimes my girl dinners me, though I'm usually over there way after eating time. Lucy. She can do steak bits in a pie."

The two agreed that Lloyd would cook their supper three nights a week. Once Tom got home, he would shower and change into shorts and a T to sit at the kitchen table nursing a Löwenbräu in a ceramic mug with his name on it. Lloyd would play chef, occasionally coming out of the kitchen to trade opinions with Tom over local events.

Tom was easy to cook for: he liked everything. Sometimes Lloyd would fetch chicken cutlets from the hot-food salad bar in the mall across the road, adding crusted rice and a green salad. Or he would platter up the parts of make-your-own BLTs, Tom's favorite.

"I didn't know you could order this at home," Tom would say, chomping into a rickety pileup of eight slices of bacon, three of tomato, and lettuce in passing. "I guess it's weird, one guy cooking for another. My old pal Jake would score us off as a pair of degenerate characters."

Lloyd's BLT was evenly balanced and cut into quarters. This allowed him to wax philosophical.

"Why are so many people," Lloyd asks, "instinctively hostile to anything they're not already used to? You mention some new thing and most folks put it down or wave it away."

"Let me try you on something," Tom replies. "Are you comfortable with novelties? Don't you really just like what you're used to, like everyone else?"

"But surprise is our education. The smarter you get, the younger you stay. Oh, wait—is there a column in that?" Grabbing his pad and pen, Lloyd hastily jots down a few words while expanding on his theme with "And the older you get, Tom, my man…yes…just let me…is the sooner you will go all befuddled…and grouchy about everything…" Note taken, Lloyd snaps back with "Right! You've got to maintain your curiosity about things to the end. It's like exercising a muscle."

After a swallow of beer from his mug, Tom fixes Lloyd with a wry look and says, "'Are you comfortable with novelties?' was a yes or no question, Lloyd, my man."

Then, one day, Lloyd found tall, stemmed glasses in the garage and made frozen parfaits in them: chocolate and strawberry ice cream, fresh peaches, and nuts on top. There were six, and when Tom found them he ate the set.

"Tom!" cried Lloyd, laughing. "They're supposed to go one at a time."

"It's my house," Tom answered. He was laughing, too.

Lloyd was fucking Portia in the spare bedroom just off the pool palace. Is this me? he wondered, or is it the latest Australian action-hero hunk scoring a fan in his trailer? Well, Lloyd did call her "My sweet" at one point, with Hollywood tang. Or does she prefer a bit of the rough stuff? Men never know what women want because women don't know themselves, except in the most abstract way: someone who'll make them feel the way their father did when they were four years old, sheltered by his protectiveness and power. The man who can inspire that feeling can have any woman he wants. Or so Lloyd imagines.

He thought he was admirably adroit in getting the condom on, but Portia calmly pulled it off and replaced it with one of her preference, some rich brand. These kids enjoy their wealth even during sex.

She rules through beauty, Lloyd thought

fleetingly, as he sought to create something compelling out of the skin-on-skin. Suddenly, she achieved, soundlessly, her head flung back, shaking wildly then abruptly still. She gently pushed him back a bit, but she was not yet done. Pulling the rubber off him with a whispered "But warn me before the flood, dearheart," she got her mouth on him. It was as if she was using Lloyd to visit where he had been, unbearably close, purest Portia there—yes, he thought, just like that—and she let out a little coo as if she could taste the very spot. The thought of it sent him flying straight off the ski jump, kicking in the air, crying, "*Now*, Portia," and she zipped out of range.

She counted, too, assessing Lloyd with "Seven, my fine fellow of the night. The first four were quite grand, too. Junior dribbles. Clark's way the most, but he always makes such a commotion."

Lloyd scarcely heard, panting in his comedown, but he did mark her smiling at him in that fashionable Portia way. The perfect hostess, securing comfort for her guests. Another petit four, Lord Misbegot?

They rested, side by side. The usual. Then she told him, "The final scene is where we get our suits back on, race out, and crash into the pool. That way, we don't smell of sex."

"But they must know what—"

She gently laid a finger on his lips. Hush. "It's good form." A half-smile. "We keep it light."

In the event, none of the others said anything to them, though Annamarie came running up to fling herself into the water by Portia's side. As always, by eleven o'clock or so the outer social loops had given way and gone home, leaving just the two girls, the two boys, and Lloyd.

Playing Truth or Dare, they gave the first question to Clark. He asked Lloyd whom of his own gender he'd have sex with. "I wouldn't," Lloyd answered.

Clark insisted. "You have to pick at least one."

"You should ask me that," Junior put in. "I have a short list all worked out. First, that smiley Fox News guy with the horn rims. Second—"

"Jennifer Anniston!" said Annamarie.

"And Gwyneth Paltrow!" said Portia.

"I want to hear from Lloyd," said Clark, with his mischievous face on. "A movie star? An athlete?"

Lloyd said nothing.

"Come on, Lloyd," Junior urged him. "Bisex is the utter mode. Everybody's doing it!"

"I won't tell your girl friend," said Clark, "if you won't tell mine."

So saying, Clark jumped up to pull something out from behind one of the chaises longues—a Canon camcorder, total zoom, top of the line. As he hefted it to his shoulder, Lloyd came toward him with "Clark! Take it away! *Now*!"

"Clark, how *dare* you?" cried Annamarie, as Lloyd, with a sense of mission the others had never seen on him before, separated Clark from the camera, telling him, "That thing goes outside or you are a guy in big trouble!"

Portia was shaking her head. "You beast, Clark! Wait till I tell Daddy!"

"Clark hopes to create a lovely video greeting card," said Clark, as Lloyd escorted him with extreme prejudice down the length of the pool to the coat room, "only to discover that his art is unappreciated. What are you," he added to Lloyd as they traveled, "a hall monitor? I hear they have them in public schools."

"Out!"

The other three were on their feet, cheering. "It was bound to happen," Junior told the girls.

"Daddy always warns me about equipment in the house," Portia was saying. "That's how he puts it, but you know Daddy. *Equipment*. He just will not have it, my dears." To Lloyd, now returning from the coat room and the confiscation of the camera, she added, "Daddy will be so pleased with you, Lloyd."

Checking his watch, Lloyd said, "I have to go."

"Not now!"

Lloyd pulled out his second copyrighted smile, the rueful boyish one. In the movie, it prompts someone to tousle your hair.

"Why so early, dude?" asked Junior while Lloyd kissed the girls goodbye.

"It's not early, and on my bike it's fifteen minutes door to door."

"If you wait for the chauffeur run," said Annamarie, "we'll drop you first."

"Charles can get the car out on two minutes' warning," Portia added.

They always say that. But then it turns out that Charles may not be on duty that night, or the car is in the shop, and suddenly the world is made of too many incongruent agendas at war with one other.

"I've got a brother," said Lloyd, who could fable his way into or out of virtually anything. "He runs the house and he's strict with me. It's a midnight curfew."

"Yeah, Cinderello!" cried Clark, from across the

pool. He hadn't rejoined the gang after his defeat with the video camera. Sulking. "Better get on your wheels and pedal away, huh?"

If I were to vanish tomorrow, would they even notice? Remember that guy from the paper? Whatever happened to him, anyone?

Tom had a habit of looking in on Lloyd before turning in. Lloyd figured that Tom was checking to see if Lloyd had respected the house rules. In fact, Tom was making sure that Lloyd was safe at home; or Tom would worry. Lloyd doesn't know this yet.

Most usually, Lloyd would be working at his computer or reading in the armchair when Tom showed up, toweling off after the extra shower he would take just before lights out. He said he loved the feel of a scrubbed-clean body against the sheets. Lloyd wasn't used to men so blunt about showing skin, and he was amused when Tom would cross the room and stand next to him, looking over Lloyd's shoulder at the Word screen as if teasing Lloyd with his manhood. Was Tom testing Lloyd in some way? Just joking around on the cutting edge? Or was he simply a natural, innocent of social cautions?

One night, Tom came by after Lloyd had gone to bed, as always leaving the door ajar and the hall light on. Seeing Tom hulking in the doorway, Lloyd sat up and startled him with "Tom, have you ever thought of building a model railroad yourself?"

"That's a sizable order," said Tom, coming over to Lloyd. "It's years of work and a hell of money to spend. All that for a big toy?"

"Okay, Tom."

"No, wait," as Tom moved closer. "It'd be the works, sure. Lovely stuff. Nice for Lucy's kids to see, off at summer camp now just, but you'll meet them in September. Ella Kate and Evan, sharp little guys. But the time for trains is past. I'm too big."

"I'm not too old for trains, Tom. And I'm older than you are."

"Yeah?" said Tom, sitting on the edge of the bed. "How old?"

"I thought we could...well, lay in some lumber and build a table. And then, bit by bit...and you've got that beautiful workspace in the garage."

Tom nodded in the semi-darkness, a suddenly faraway Tom. The hall light loved his skin and he glistened.

Then Tom said, "Plywood sheets, I guess. Four by eights are best. That what your layout was mounted on? At the orphanage?"

"Who knows? We never thought about it."

Tom nodded again. "Kids don't know what anything's made of. The content of things. They can be irresponsible, which I don't approve of. Yeah, so...you score tonight? At the rich kids'? What's that girl's name?"

"Portia."

"Spicy?"

"Very appealing. But not sexy in the porn-star sense."

Lloyd shifted his weight so he could lie flat on his back, disheveling the covers. Tom righted them, pulling them up to Lloyd's shoulders.

"She's a bit brisk," Lloyd went on. "The sex, I

mean. Really young but very experienced. She knows exactly what she wants from a man. And she doesn't kiss all that much. Sometimes not at all."

"Never heard of that," said Tom. "Girls live to kiss and kiss to live."

"Not Portia."

"All those rich kids are different, I guess. They all have cars? Bought by daddy?"

Lloyd nodded.

"Didn't I know it?" Tom said, laying one hand flat on the covers over Lloyd's chest. "But don't go riding in those vehicles after hours, now, because they'll attract law enforcement with a dead taillight or not signaling or just generally being selfish rich kids. Stop the vehicle for a violation means search it. Yeah, and what do we find? *Substance*. Okay, who belongs to that? And the rich kids point at you with 'Him, officer!' Don't relish being called to bail you out of jail some night for rebellious behavior."

"I'll be careful, Tom."

"And write the contact intel for that rich kids place for me and leave it under one of the fridge magnets, in case of...you know. Some eventuality. You're always going over there, sure. It's right to be a part of something. Membership in it, a guy they respect. Sure. But then you always want to return to the place that's yours. Feeling your breathing under my hand like this, like to know you're home and happy now."

They paused there, and then Tom rose and folded the edges of the bedclothes in between the mattress and the box spring.

"Tuck you in," said Tom, "so you'll rest easy.

Get you off to a solid start come morning."

As Tom leaned over to even out the lie of the blanket, his yellow hair brushed Lloyd's forehead. Then Tom stretched to his full six feet four inches and left the room.

Tom had an old buddy named Jake, and Lloyd couldn't stand him. It was an odd pairing, Lloyd thought, because Jake was closer in age to Lloyd than to Tom, yet Tom claimed he and Jake went "all the way back to milk and cookies." There was only one thing to know about Jake: he didn't own a television. That meant he had to come to Tom's on certain weekends to watch The Game.

There was always a Game, and enthusiasm about the teams, and a whole encyclopedia of bygone Games and famous players. Lloyd found it as tedious as hearing realtors talk rents, and he suffered an evil close encounter when his editor suggested a column or two on local high-school teams. Lloyd insisted on leaving sports to the paper's sports guys.

On the other hand, Jake would provision an amusing column, if Lloyd could bear writing about him: a noisy galoot in a Stetson who made obnoxious jokes. Whenever Jake was to be around Tom's girl, Lucy, Jake had to promise—solemnly, on their friendship itself—that he would behave.

"And my old Jake will keep that promise for just about two hours," Tom explained to Lloyd. "Then it's a pure case of Dam is bust, head for the hills!"

It was typical of Jake that he was never actually introduced to Lloyd: Jake simply pushed open Lloyd's door to barge in and snarl, "This is the Eurozone secret police. Are you hiding a woman in this room?"

At his desk, Lloyd turned in alarm just as Tom came in.

"This your new sidekick?" Jake asked Tom. "He's pretty."

"Pay him no mind," Tom advised Lloyd.

"You know what they call a pretty guy where I come from?" Jake asked Lloyd.

"Cut it out, Jake," said Tom, though he was grinning.

Getting too close to Lloyd, Jake went on, "They call you 'wife-stealer.' Hear it? Since you're the kind that…*what*? I'm only—"

"Don't be getting in his face and scaring him up," said Tom, who had grabbed Jake's arm to pull him away. "He doesn't know about your jokes."

"A date snatch if I ever seen one," said Jake, never taking his eyes off Lloyd as he allowed Tom to drag him to the door.

"No, he's a classic fellow with a college style that's way over your head. Now, you come on to the TV and get the beer drunk, so you can get all melancholy instead of fighting with every guy you see, in the good old Jake manner."

To Lloyd, as they departed, Tom added, "If I had a buck for every bar they threw this lug out of…Say, you want to watch the game with us, pal? There's beer enough for a squad."

"I think I'll get in a bike ride till Bizarro World is over," said Lloyd.

"I think I'll put on a speckled vest and loafers and get in some cocksucking," Jake snorted back. "Who'll put a penny in my loafers?"

"Come on, troublemaker," said Tom as the two disappeared.

Outside, in the breezy summer-fall heat, Lloyd made an afternoon of it. Between laps, he had a sandwich and chatted up members of a women's cycling club lounging on a break in the city park running along Northside. When Lloyd got back, quite some time later, Tom was by himself at the kitchen table, reading the paper as he finished off a beer.

"Here's a nice column of yours," Tom announced. He held the paper up to show Lloyd. "Makes me feel important to know a guy with his name so standout in the press. Reading all about the trendy new swimming strokes and bathing wear. That'll be handy if the *Titanic* goes down again."

"Is Nosferatu gone?" asked Lloyd, parking his bike helmet on what Tom referred to as "the step thing": an old high chair with a fold-in ladder attachment.

"Old Jake likes you," said Tom, with the look of a child getting into an inspired bit of mischief. "He plans to flirt and tease you fiercely, maybe corner you at a Christmas party when you're in a Santa suit and take it off you piece by piece. Yeah, old Jake's got ideas about you. And none of your faces, now, when I'm just telling what old Jake said."

Getting a water bottle out of the fridge, Lloyd said, "It's not fair to joke at me so radically."

"Can't help it if you're his type, can I?"

"His type of what?" Lloyd replied, sitting across from Tom and taking a swig of water.

Shaking his head in mock-concern, Tom said,

"Old Jake would know just what to do with a rebellious desperado like yourself, I can tell you that. He would whisper his schemes for you while tenderizing you all at once."

"Tom!" cried Lloyd, half-scandalized.

Tom started to heft his mug for another swallow, decided against it, looked at Lloyd and slipped into that naughty-boy grin once more. "My old Jake? He would flirt and tease you for certain. Favorite trick's where you're on the phone to break a date with your chick, and while you're talking Jake's all over you, pulling off your clothes and smooching away all over the place. He'll eat up your johnson, too. Does the chick catch on? If she does, you lose and Jake gets to score you big time."

No longer startled, Lloyd was playing it on the casual side. Finishing off his water as if Tom had been recounting a movie plot, Lloyd asked, "But what if I win?"

"You get out in one piece."

Again, Tom grasped his mug as if to raise it but didn't follow through.

"Jake asked if he could have you for a night," he said.

"What?"

"Don't worry. If anyone gets to rough you over it's me, when I punish you for your crimes."

In his suave mode, Lloyd carefully screwed the top back on the empty water bottle, set it on the table, leaned toward Tom, and said, "Okay if it comes to that, whatever that actually is. But I don't like you getting radical just to get a rise out of me."

Tom chuckled.

Wait a minute. "Tom…are you drunk?"

"It's well-meant in spirit," Tom replied, stumbling just a bit over the words. "My old Jake and his nutty fun. He can be disorderly, sure. Told him not to…you know, bust into your room. Does it anyway, Jake. But you can count on that man for certain. Saved my life more than once, I can tell you."

"He saved your life? How?"

Tom got to his feet, using the table for support, and started unsteadily toward his room.

"Tom," Lloyd began, also rising, but Tom waved him back.

"Don't need help," he said.

Sure enough, Tom got to his bed without mishap. There he passed out fully dressed and didn't reappear till three hours later. He had showered and changed and seemed completely recovered; Lloyd found him rummaging in the fridge.

"Ever since you came," Tom said, agreeably, "I don't know what any of the food is."

"Sit down and I'll fix you something."

"Overshot my bolt," said Tom, taking a chair at the big round table.

"Who won? The game, I mean," said Lloyd, starting a plate at the kitchen counter.

After a bit, Tom replied, "Don't rightly remember." He stopped there, finally adding, "That's a bad sign, blacking out."

"You're entitled to slide every so often, I suppose."

"My daddy sure wouldn't say so."

Lloyd poked around in the fridge, pulled out cutlery and napkins, unwrapped, washed, arranged.

Tom looked on silently for a while, then said, "Jake really got to you, huh?"

"It takes all kinds."

"Yeah, he's not to every taste, old Jake. It's like, there are various people you'd rather be with, because of being polite and enjoyable. But who knows if you can depend on them when you're in trouble? That's how I judge."

Lloyd went on working in silence, then set down a plate for Tom: quartered Courtland apples, St. André cheese, and Carr's biscuits.

"Now what?" asked Tom.

"They opened a cheese and fruit store in the mall yesterday," said Lloyd, sitting across from Tom with a cup of coffee from the pot that hummed all day. "It was one of those galas, with discounts and a local dignitary and tasting kiosks."

"What's that mean?" asked Tom, poking at the food with his fork.

"Free samples."

"Okay, but why is it apples with cheese?"

"Tom, you are so…look. Just…just try it."

"Okay, boss."

"Boy. Now who's rebellious?"

Silence as Tom cuts and forks up the apple slices and smears gobs of cheese onto biscuits.

"This is good," he says at last. "Why are you so nice to me?"

Lloyd just sits there while Tom cleans his plate.

"I really liked that," he says. "Is this how your friends eat? The rich kids?"

"Yes, in fact."

"Lucy doesn't know about it. I'll have to tell her.

Just a half-cup": because Lloyd was pouring him some coffee. "Do they know about me? Your friends."

"They think you're my brother."

"Well, there's a puzzle."

Placing the milk carton and the sugar bowl next to Tom's coffee, Lloyd said, "They were ragging on me for having a curfew, so I alibied. Living with my brother. He's old-fashioned and he owns the house…you know."

"Guess I am, at that. Old-fashioned. 'Cause of the family I come from." Tasting his brew, Tom added, "This coffee really hits the spot after a heavy day."

"It's funny to see you take it without a donut," said Lloyd, stowing the milk and sugar. "They may drum you out of the cops' union. Only we're out of… What's wrong?"

Tom was on his feet, staring at Lloyd with a look of angry suspicion.

Lloyd froze.

"You come with me," Tom told him. "*Now*."

"Come…where?"

Without responding, Tom turned and started off, and after a moment Lloyd followed. They entered Tom's room, where Tom told Lloyd to sit on the bed. Looming over him, Tom said, "How did you know I was a cop?"

Perplexed, Lloyd answered, "Didn't you tell me?"

"No. I did not tell you."

Tom looked hard and implacable.

"I did *not* tell you," he repeated.

"Well, I…I must have figured it out is all. Though I don't remember one certain moment where

I…But your attitudes are cop. The things you say are cop. Only where do they find uniforms big enough for you?"

"They have them," Tom allowed.

"Do I have to sit before you like a felon under interrogation?"

Tom extended a hand to pull Lloyd up.

"No, I want to get up by myself."

"Told you, I don't like you rebellious."

So Lloyd said, "Okay, Tom," took his hand, and was on his feet again.

"For instance," Lloyd continued, "Americans say 'car' or 'truck.' But you say 'vehicle,' as in 'Step away from the...' Or when you warned me not to ride with my friends and get arrested. Who would think of that but a cop?"

Tom was mulling it over.

"Besides," Lloyd concluded, "you know how you love donuts and coffee."

Tom didn't react, so Lloyd tried this: he placed his right hand on Tom's left shoulder, patted the muscle, and then said, "You can trust me, Tom."

Tom nodded slightly.

"Log line," Lloyd announced. "Cool, take-charge action hero opens a room of his house to a lively stranger, only to discover that opening up has its risks."

Tom turned, walked to his closet, and pulled back the door, revealing three tour suits and one more elaborate one, presumably the dress uniform.

"I thought you'd been snooping," Tom explained. "You saw this stuff and that was how you know."

Lloyd was stunned. "Tom, I would *never* do that

to you! Snooping is…It's…But why didn't you just tell me you were a cop?"

"It's a sensitive issue. 'Cause civilians don't understand what it's about, and they are apt to speak scornfully."

Shutting the closet door, Tom went on, "My daddy was a cop. He raised four kids with encouragement for us, though he knew that kids are reckless by nature and yearned to punish the disobedience out of us. He was too rough on my sisters, I admit. But my brother and I could take it."

"What would he do?"

"It'd be too extreme to talk of nowadays in our society of whiners. Going to show you something now."

Tom led Lloyd through the house to the place that was always barred: his father's old bedroom. Pausing just slightly in his thoughts, Tom then pushed in, taking Lloyd along with a hand on his arm.

The room was a double of Tom's—the father of it, one might say. There was the same bureau and (empty) water jug, the same bedclothes, the same desk piled with books. Even the closet, when Tom opened it up to Lloyd, held the same uniforms.

"I'm as strict as my daddy was," said Tom, turning to Lloyd as he gently shut the closet door. "Or I will be, when I have kids in tow. I know how to correct the wildness, 'cause if you don't they'll end in trouble good."

As he spoke, Tom moved slowly about the room, occasionally stopping to feel the surfaces and corners of its parts.

"You've heard me joke about my old pal Jake and

his radical methods with a guy he likes. He needs a challenge from certain young fellas. Wild ones, like. Takes them up like one of your fad hobbies, old Jake, to see how effective his disciplines will be on the different types. The secret thief. Or the jock, full of his sarcasms. Rowdy characters, to be sure."

Looking over the books on the desk, Lloyd said, "Tom, I will not let you shock me with your crazy stories. I don't think any of them are even…*Tom*! Here, these…these are…" Excited, Lloyd picked up one, a second, a third. "They're your model railroading books! *This* is where you keep them? In your father's room? But it was he who wouldn't let you build a train set. Right?"

Tom didn't say anything.

"Why are they here, Tom?"

"I don't know," Tom replied: and he really didn't. Sitting on the bed, he motioned for Lloyd to join him, and, as Lloyd sat, Tom said, "My brother and I wanted a layout so much. It was the only time my daddy let us down, though I understand it now. And here's you, with no daddy, in the orphanage. Yet you had a model railroad just the same. So who of us came out ahead?"

Lloyd kept it light and conversational: "Did you see the clip on television about the soldier who came home on leave from Iraq and dropped in on his little boy at school as a surprise? The boy was five or six, there in class with his schoolmates. He looks up and…there is his father. In full uniform, this is, and they haven't seen each other in who knows how long. That's an epoch to someone so young. And daddy's right there, out of…magic, standing there in his…costume of valor, you might say. Smiling at his little boy. Who doesn't smile back, or say anything, but just…goes straight to his dad. Right up to him with a…helpless joy. A kind of grownup resolve. And that soldier dad scoops him up in his arms so the boy can hold on to his protector. Just hold on to him there. It's all that little boy knows about at that moment—his love for his dad and his certainty that his dad loves him just as much. That very much, right there. That much."

After a bit, Tom asked, "What did the soldier look like? Dressed for war? Tough about it? A tall guy?"

"You know, I didn't see him, really. I mean, he was there, but I…I got mesmerized by the intensity of the little boy. To be so *sure* of someone. So close to him. Father James used to visit us every night at lights out, going from bed to bed and asking about our day. Like, you know, How is the music coming along, or Sister says you're making great progress. He meant well, but he really couldn't tell us apart. He'd ask how my garden was doing. We'll all be so grateful for those vegetables. But, no, Father, it's *Lonnie's* garden, and, besides, we all make fun of him, because guys don't have gardens. And you, John Mary, did you finish your scrapbook on those movie stars? And we were like, That isn't even Lonnie. *What* scrapbook?"

Lloyd stopped there, and Tom told him, very gently, "You've got no kick coming. They took care of you, at least. Some real-life parents don't do that. I see it every day on the job."

"I'm not kicking, Tom."

"Good, then."

They sat there for a while after that, watching the

sun move shadows through the room as it set for the day.

Summer was ending, and for the Portias it was off to being either Adults With Career Plans or Rich Wastrels.

"Can you picture Clark filling out his résumé?" Annamarie asked the gang as they picked at a vast platter of tacos and toppings.

Clark pictured it: "Education: expensive but worthless. Job: vampire."

"Now me," said Junior. "Job: paid escort to the stars."

It was one of the most crowded parties Lloyd had ever been to at Portia's, with many guests he had never seen before. There were odd people, plain people, even old people: not a strictly Portia crowd. Lloyd wondered if, somehow or other, Portia's parents had been permitted to fold their personal guest list into Portia's; he kept having to be introduced to people with last names.

And then a total stranger got up in Lloyd's face, in one of those "That's right, I'm just going to do this you" actions. This man managed to be both effeminate and nondescript (a type, Lloyd had learned long before, that always meant trouble), and he materialized out of nowhere to push himself on Lloyd with "Yes, you're the one who lives with that *magnificent* policeman!"

"I am?" said Lloyd, with a bland smile. He maintained a quota on conversations with troublemakers—zero for life—and he immediately started to amble off.

"Don't you high-hat *me*, Miss Cute!" the man snarled, following Lloyd.

Lloyd continued to move away, his smile as fixed as a bayonet, so the man grabbed his arm.

"Scared of what you'll hear, Dewdrop?" he murmured, right into Lloyd's ear. "I have the address and attention of everyone who matters in this town."

It was a remark designed to stop you, turn you back to hear more. A movie line, you might say: forcing the scene to continue. But Lloyd kept traveling. He caught sight of Junior all alone by the pool house and made him his goal as the man now started shouting behind Lloyd's back.

"Wait till the other cops find out you're boy friends! How they do love a queer romance!"

And Junior, grinning for scandal as Lloyd reached him, said, "What was that about, dude?"

Lloyd shrugged. "Who is that, anyway?"

"We call him Realtor Guy. He does the screenings for Portia's dad's buildings."

"Nasty character," Lloyd remarked.

"He never stays long."

Whoever he was, he didn't approach Lloyd again. It was easy to get lost in the crowd tonight—but Clark, that gleeful showboater, commanded the room with a spot of exhibition dancing, his swimsuit sagging below the decency level.

"It's a contest!" he announced, though as usual no one troubled to establish any rules. Most of the younger guests took part, including Lloyd; somebody's uncle was the judge. Junior won, and was quite agog. He even forgot to say, "It was bound to happen."

Then Portia led Lloyd away from the others with a proprietary, confidential air. "Daddy just loves that you made Clark lose the camera," she told him. "Looking out for the sanctity of the homestead."

Amused, Lloyd said, "You told him about that?"

"Daddy's favorite tells Daddy everything," she replied, pulling Lloyd into the side room she used for sex. "There are no secrets from Daddy, and that is how he keeps his love close."

"I like secrets," said Lloyd, as she pulled off his Speedos. "They keep relationships pure. You and I have a very pure relationship, wouldn't you say? Portia?"

She was getting out that rich brand of condom, waiting as he worked himself up for her. She wasn't listening. Through the door, he could hear the party getting livelier, drunker.

"I would like to do a column about you, Portia," he said, as she got her mouth on him for a long slow catch right to the base, looking up at his face all the while. A champ at this.

"Just on you, Portia," he went on. "Would you like that? A…kind of…yes, salute to…a young woman of, I would say, great, great—"

"Don't be tiresome, Lloyd," she said, interrupting her incantatory navigations. "There's nothing less fascinating than a summer toy at the end of the summer."

Biking home well in advance of curfew, Lloyd went right into his room and booted up to knock off the outline for the novel he was always threatening to write. Maybe one about an orphan from nowhere who cracks a loop of moneyed don'tcares in a midwestern city. A summer toy. And this novel will be called *The Rules*: because he breaks them all and wins the girl and is respected and beloved and his novel makes a fortune. For once in his uneventful life. He passes a tart inspection by the girl's derisive mother—a great scene!—to thrive as favored son-in-law, decisive and strong. No *equipment* at the pool, you hear? Camera, begone! No evidence, you see. Fly lightly through the world. And as time goes on the summer toy turns into a don'tcare himself, even as he fears the dark and the future.

"See, you're right where you should be at this hour," said Tom, looking in at the doorway, nude as usual. "Compliance," he added. "Respect for others."

"Tom, you are always joking in such weird ways."

"Not joking now," said Tom, and he went off down the hall.

No, wait, I have something here, Lloyd thought, developing his outline with picturesque incidentals. Writing all those columns taught Lloyd to give the reader the necessary data. When, where, who, and what does everyone look like? Young and pretty? And when are they lying? When aren't they? Are they even real? It's a dream, isn't it? all that money and easy living and you at the edge of it, staring at the inside, tranquilizing worries with a fantasy. Father James told us orphans are chosen by God, to test the bounds of human compassion. Too bad we don't test the bounds of social class. You know what class you are? You're a tiresome summer toy who thought looks and charm would whisk you past the door guy. Cinderello makes a hit at the ball only to discover that Lloyd was weeping uncontrollably, even sobbing in great tortured helpings of surrender to the same old nameless fears, staring at himself in the mirror mounted along the top of the bureau, wiping his eyes with his sleeve. It was bound to happen: mapping around from job to job, four years short of forty, and you just aren't going to make it ever, are you? Then he sees the reflection of Tom, staring at him from the doorway.

"What's the matter?" asked Tom, in his brusque way, the nervy cock swinging as he comes closer, curious. Lloyd's reddened face in the glass, too, wet sleeve, messed hair, reddened face. A little breakdown.

"I thought you'd gone to bed," Lloyd got out, as he turned to face Tom.

"Let's go," Tom ordered, taking hold of Lloyd's right arm.

"Don't arrest me," said Lloyd. Was that a jest?

Tom guided Lloyd through the house to Tom's bathroom, washed Lloyd's face and made him brush his teeth, then took Lloyd into the bedroom.

"Get stripped," Tom told him. "Don't like the feel of clothes in bed."

"I'm thirsty." Stalling, Lloyd?

Tom poured Lloyd a glass of water from his night jug. As Lloyd drank, Tom said, "F'you're like this tonight, what'll you be like at Christmas?"

Handing the glass back to Tom, Lloyd pulled off his clothes, saying, "Christmas isn't the problem."

"Scoot on in," said Tom, pulling back the bedclothes. "You'll be next to the wall."

Tossing Lloyd a spare pillow from the closet and switching off the light, Tom joined Lloyd in bed and evened the covers over the two of them. Then, settling in, he said, "Okay. Want to tell me now?"

Abashed, Lloyd buried his face in his pillow and husked out a no.

"Rebellious as ever," said Tom. "No one gets to sympathize with me, *no* sir!"

There followed a silence, apparently an eloquent one, for Lloyd saw Tom watching him as if listening.

Finally, his voice muffled in the pillow, Lloyd got out, "I'm a flop, Tom."

"What at?"

Changing the subject, Lloyd asked, "How come you always finish off the day here? Why do you never sleep over with Lucy?"

"Don't like to rest in someone else's bed."

"Wouldn't she like you to stay over?"

"Course. All women like you to stay over."

"Are you going to marry her, Tom?"

"Wasn't this about you, pal?"

After a bit, Lloyd said, "Yes, Tom. Except." And left it at that.

"Something else," said Tom. "Would you be willing to teach Lucy your recipe for that dinner with the fish sticks and spaghetti? Her sauce isn't the way I like."

"Sure, Tom."

"Thought I'd have her over next time my old Jake's here for a game. She doesn't care for his ways any more than you do, but he's my oldest buddy, so everyone can just get used to him. And meanwhile, you could make that dish while Lucy watches."

Turning around to face the world again, Lloyd said, "I'd be glad to. I'd like to meet her."

"You going to tell me a secret? Why do you still always agree when I ask for something? After all this time! You aren't hardly rebellious at all is the truth. Lucy, too. But everyone else gives me arguments all the day long, whether they're on my side or no. Right. And now, buddy boy…" Shifting his weight to look hard at Lloyd, Tom asked, "You going to trust me enough to say why you were losing it in your room before?"

"I don't want to, Tom."

"Well, anyway…Been thinking about this a bit." Tom rested his hand on Lloyd's head, waggled it a bit, then said, "What would you say to setting up our own model railroad? One of those fancy layouts, with all the things we've talked about."

Lloyd abruptly turned to Tom, grasping his hand as he took it off Lloyd's head. "I would *love* that, Tom! We could build a table and start constructing the thing step by step! I bet we could have a start-up oval, the first bits of a town, and a mountain and tunnel in days!"

In the light from the hallway, Lloyd could see silent Tom grinning.

"Although," Lloyd went on, "where would we put it? That empty room by the back door? What do you call that?"

"That's the porch. Or it was going to be, for summer afternoons with lemonade and children's funny little questions when they try to get smarter. It was my daddy's project, but he was always too busy, and then…"

Silence.

"Couldn't build a train set there, anyway. The carpet throws up tiny textile germs, get into the wheels and track lines. Jam the whole system up."

Another silence. Lloyd coughed.

"Tell you what—I've been thinking of opening up my daddy's room. He liked a solid wood floor, without a frill, as you maybe noticed. We could move the furniture out and build the table there. Guess it's time, anyway. Finally."

"Wow."

"You've probably noticed that big department store downtown, quick by City Hall. With the turret, like a castle? It's an official landmark, makes us all proud and teary-eyed. O'Connor and Deal's Hardware and Trade. Been there forever with that lovely title. Folks just call it 'The Hardware.' Well, sir, that is the place in all the territory for model railroading—parts, kits, a whole section just on locomotives. They even hire out a specialist to advise you if you have wiring problems or the like. Least, they used to. One of the last places of the kind, I believe. We could take a look at what they've got, make some plans. Organization. Discussion. When I was a kid, we called it 'looking at the trains in The Hardware.' My daddy would take us, though he disapproved. He knew how hungry we were to know of it."

"Tom," said Lloyd, "you must be one amazing cop."

"The hell you say," answered Tom, agreeably.

They fell silent again, and then they went to sleep.

From that night on, Lloyd and Tom bunked next to each other in Tom's bed: chaste as icons on a desktop but close, close. Lloyd continued to excite commentary from the Portias when, about half after eleven o'clock, he would take leave of them to bike home for his curfew.

So the summer toy was still playing with the rich kids. He shouldn't have been; where is his pride? But he found them charming, irresistibly so. He liked the swimming and the food. He liked feeling that he had found a niche among the young and beautiful: an orphan finds a niche but seldom in this world. Then, too, knowing a variety of people gives one writing material. But Lloyd was always glad to get back to his own address, to the look of amused suspicion on Tom's face when Lloyd walked in and "What misdemeanors did you and those friends get into tonight?" The two would take turns brushing their teeth in the mirror of Tom's bathroom, and Tom would tease Lloyd. "If Jake was here," he might say, "I guess he would know just what to do with a certain handsome fellow I know."

And Lloyd would reply, "Tom, not again!"

"Jake's a devil," Tom chuckles, taking the toothbrush from Lloyd and washing it for him, because he says Lloyd doesn't do a thorough job, and you don't want any fleas getting into the bristles.

"A devil?" Lloyd echoed. "Jake's a demented clown whom you defend simply because you went to Sunday school together." Moving into the bedroom. "Or whatever it was."

"Jake's a solid man," says Tom, pulling down the

bedcovers. “Those in trouble can turn to the Jakes of this world, and no others.”

“I wouldn’t turn to Jake,” says Lloyd, sliding over to the wall side of the bed.

And Tom says, “You’re going to turn to me.”

Lloyd was in his room writing his next column for the paper when Lucy and her kids arrived. The column, another look at courtship rituals in Lloyd’s gym, was going too well for him to break off, though he would have liked to collect the moment when Tom greeted his girl. Gruffly affectionate? Deeply enamored? A fleeting kiss and a grin, romance in business casual?

When Lloyd finally came out, six-year-old Ella Kate and four-year-old Evan were following Tom around to tell him things. It was clearly their habit whenever they saw Tom, and he just as clearly enjoyed giving them attention. Interestingly, he didn’t adopt the distant yes-yes grownup response to children, but actually listened to them. He even drew them out, no matter what the topic. When Evan described a dream he had, Tom gave him so much ego-gratification dialogue on it that Evan immediately began to tell of another dream.

“He’s making it up!” Ella Kate cried. She wasn’t resentful: she just liked announcing things.

Immediately after the introductions, Lloyd palmed a quarter and extended both fists to Ella Kate. Manipulating the coin from hand to hand, he then told her, “Guess where it is and it’s yours.”

She guessed wrong.

"How about you, young man?" Lloyd asked Evan, an avid witness to all this.

Evan guessed wrong, too.

Tom and Lucy were looking on.

"There's a trick to it." Lloyd showed them: "First, you juggle it back and forth, very obviously. See? Then you appear to make a final transfer…and…watch how I push my left fist against my right while opening my right hand up. See that? And I'm staring down at my right fist as if accidentally giving my strategy away. But it's all a hoax."

Lloyd opened the empty right fist to show them.

"Now, who wants to try it?"

Then Jake came in with "Those kids again!"

Tom laughed. He thought everything Jake did was the height of drollery, even Jake's heading right to the living-room couch to watch nonsense on the television (with the volume off), as if trying to will the pre-game to start.

But then Jake had to give up the couch, because Lloyd decided to host *The Ella Kate and Evan Show*, featuring Ella Kate and Evan's guests, Tom, Lucy, and Jake.

"No way," Jake growled, glaring from a chair.

"It's a television talk show!" Ella Kate announced.

"What do we talk about?" asked Evan, who was going to make his broadcast debut still holding his glass of tomato juice.

"The topic is school," said Lucy.

Ella Kate and Evan settled on the couch, and Ella Kate launched the talk with "First grade can be all so gloomy at times."

"What's gloomy about it?" Jake rasped.

"No heckling from the studio audience," said Lloyd.

"Yeah? Well, then, *you* say how first grade is gloomy!"

"Evan," Lucy put in, "why don't you tell us about your school experiences."

"I go to Gymble," said Evan, in the tone you use for "I'm getting my bachelor's degree at Yale University."

"Gymble isn't school," Ella Kate announced to the studio audience. "All they do is have playtime and get a lot of treats."

"It is, too, school," said Evan, getting worried.

"School is where they teach you to read and write. They don't teach anything at Gymble."

"Yes, they *did* tell us," Evan insisted. Then he had to be comforted till it was time for Tom and Jake's program. Off went the kids to the porch to play with the LEGO bricks that Tom kept for these occasions. Ella Kate announced that she was building "Miss Parsnip's School for Young Brides." Evan worked on an airplane. With Tom and Jake parked on the couch in the rapt yet uproarious state in which their kind takes in The Game, Lloyd and Lucy headed into the kitchen so he could show her how to make fish sticks and spaghetti the way Tom liked it.

Now Lucy. Lloyd had greatly wondered what sort of woman could suit the redoubtable Tom, and from the moment Lloyd set eyes on her he was thinking, Of course. Attractive but not in a showy way. Smart. Spirited, too, but soft. A woman with a lot of smiling content but not one to argue over nothing just to test the response. Happy and distinctive. When she disagreed with Tom, she didn't try to topple him. She simply disagreed.

Portia and Lucy: discuss. Money makes the difference. It has spoiled Portia by freeing her. She'll never be a single mom with two kids and a day job, like Lucy. Portia doesn't know how to finesse a budget vexed with hidden costs, such as a dentist emergency or a school field trip. Portia points at what she needs and it is given to her. She can make strategic mistakes without paying for them the rest of her days; she doesn't pay beyond this Thursday.

But Lucy has a magic: she knows what everything is. Portia's men are boys who dance in Speedos. Lucy, only a few years older, has found in Tom the ideal nesting partner, because duty, in Tom, creates devotion. Aside from his work, there will be nothing in all the life of Tom but his family, as provider, source of strength, and redeemer.

Lucy said as much to Lloyd as they got the dinner things out. "Tom has his controlling side, of course," she admitted. "But he's awesome in the dependable department."

Washing a lemon, Lloyd answered, "You must have had a father like Tom. Girls who called a good man Daddy want a good man for a husband."

As Lloyd tossed the lemon in the air juggler-style, Lucy said, "Don't think they're easy to come by, either." Examining the plastic crock of grated parmesan, she asked, "Where do you get this?"

"Across the avenue, at that fancy-Dan mall. The grocery stocks gourmet items, but they're mixed in with everything else, like a secret message. The fresh stuff is right next to the package brands, but it's there."

In the living room, then two men cheered some play as Lucy gave the cheese an inquisitive shake. She nodded at Lloyd: you notice things, my friend. That I respect.

That's what she was thinking. What she *said* was "Tom is still young. Little more than a boy, really. He seems so certain about everything, but he's had very little experience in living his life. One moment, as we hold that thought..."

Lucy stepped out of the kitchen to check on her kids. They were still on the porch making their LEGO models.

"Back again," she went on, returning, while Lloyd set a large pot of water to boil. "My point is that a young man can surprise you. He can swear by his job this year and change it the next. He can light out of the state. He can fall in love."

"Right, the well-known 'king of the world' syndrome. He becomes enriched...empowered...I need another e...enlightened."

"Well done," said Lucy, of Lloyd's nimble wording. And "May I?" she asked, extending a hand to the bottle of olive oil that he pulled out of the pantry.

Lloyd gave it to her.

"The good stuff?" she asked.

"You can't cheat on the oil," Lloyd told her. "Even Tom would taste it."

"Do you think," Lucy asked, looking at Lloyd meaningfully, "that Tom will...let's say...undergo that 'king of the world' syndrome?"

"I don't know," said Lloyd, simply and honestly.

"Yes, *but*!" she went on. "Because I do have an

edge in one respect, and…oh, is this the sauce? In a store jar? After Tom's praise of this dish, I thought we'd be melting tomatoes all afternoon in mysterious herbs."

"If it costs over six bucks," said Lloyd, "it's as good as homemade."

"This is my Lucy edge," she then said. "I don't crowd him. Like…okay, here: inventing a girl. Let's call her Sheila. I've always hated that name. *Right*, so Sheila texts Tom with 'I called you seven times last night where were you why didn't you and the flowers for my mother's birthday, buster!'"

Lloyd laughed.

"And," Lucy concluded, "that's really not the girl for Tom, is it?"

"With that philosophy, I'll bet you'll prevail—no, let me": because Lucy was about to check on her kids again. Lloyd looked out instead. Ella Kate, still working with the LEGOs, had moved into the living room and Evan was napping in Tom's arms.

"They're fine," said Lloyd, coming back.

"Speaking of all that," said Lucy, taking two smallish wicker baskets out of the typical children's things bag, "how's *your* romantic life, if I may ask?"

Lloyd paused.

"Tom says you're one of those worldly guys. 'European and classic' was how he put it. He means 'classy,' of course. Still, if you'd rather not…"

"What are those, anyway?" Lloyd asked, looking at the baskets.

"We call them 'luncheon kits.' The children can't do spaghetti, so these are…" Lucy opened one: a sandwich neatly wrapped in see-through, a bag of carrot sticks, a little carton of milk, a box of raisins. "It's a trick to get them to eat healthy. I assign the sandwich, but they choose the rest, and that makes them feel grownup."

"They're delightful kids," said Lloyd, inspecting the other basket, whose electives were celery sticks, sugarless lemonade, and almonds.

"Well." She smiled, admitting the obvious. "They're always at their best on a Tom Day. Their term. I've never known anyone who didn't try to be at their best around Tom. I suspect because his disapproval is so—"

"Where's the eats?" demanded Jake, abruptly popping in.

Lloyd held up fingers at Lucy.

"Oh, I'm the…translator?" To Jake, she said, "Ten minutes."

As Jake returned to The Game, Lucy asked Lloyd, "That fast? Really? And is there something unhappy between you and Jake? Because he's just a big goof, you know."

Lloyd was sliding the dry spaghetti into the pot. "We'll broil the fish sticks in that foil pan. And what *is* Tom's disapproval, exactly?"

"Sheer damnation, trust me. Shall I open the box of…oh, good, no trans fat."

Then the secret of Lloyd's sauce: you plopped the cooked macaroni onto a bed of grated cheese, tossing it with olive oil and fresh-cracked peppercorns. But not *too* tossed, so the cheese could melt in clumps.

"Tom likes it crusty," Lloyd explained.

Showing Lucy how to decorate the dish with the tomato sauce rather than saturate it, Lloyd said, "This way, you get a soupy business with the oil at the bottom. It's a kind of dessert if you like to bread-dip."

"Right. It looks wonderful," said Lucy. "But isn't this a little like a four-star restaurant offering the blue-plate special? After all, it's just fish sticks and spaghetti."

"That's the point," Lloyd replied, as he divvied up the meal into plates for the grownups. "It's basic, but dependable."

The food was served on those folding television tables that went out of fashion everywhere but the midwest, where paper napkins are tucked into collars, where nobody mutes the sound during commercial breaks, and where Ella Kate announces, "Evan sometimes puts a carrot in his nose."

Much later, when Tom got back from Lucy's, he complimented Lloyd on making the afternoon "breezy."

"Are you going to marry Lucy?" Lloyd asked, washing while Tom dried.

"Well, now, buddy, I just might. And I just might not, so there you are."

"It's captivating to see you with her. Because you're so obviously a couple, yet you play it totally cooldown. None of those showboating bits proving your love, where you grab at each other making coo-coo noises."

Tom snorted.

"Well," said Lloyd, "some couples really get into that."

"Don't need to be in love to get married, though.

You need to be in respect. Lucy's the finest woman I know. Did you like her?"

"Very much. In the old days, she was called 'a handsome woman.' Not just for her looks, but her whole way of being. Her ease."

"You were great with the kids. Hand me that towel, this one's all…yes, that one."

"You're the guy who's great with kids," said Lloyd.

"I had a sterling example in my daddy, of course. But I heard a thing about you that I need to ask on right now. From old Jake. The realtor who's selling Jake's house for him? Seems he told Jake that you're looking for a place of your own. All of a sudden. That true?"

"I…*what*? Why is Jake getting involved in—"

"No, hold on, no one's indicting you yet. Jake's set to give up his house and take an apartment, though I make it that your house is your family, and I was careful to explain that to my old Jake there. Selling your house is like selling your kinfolk. But would he listen? You've stopped washing."

"Tom, is this another of your jokes?"

Tom looked at Lloyd as if gauging his honesty, an inquisitor reading soul.

"I asked if you were joking," Lloyd repeated.

"The answer to that is no."

"Then let's use our heads, okay? I don't have the money to move, first of all, and, second, when has Jake ever said anything that makes sense?"

"He's only reporting what he heard," said Tom, relinquishing the towel and turning off the faucet. "Since it's intermission here. But why would the realtor guy invent such a tale?"

"*What* tale?"

"That you're looking at places with an eye to move out of this house and leave me in the lurch and didn't tell me."

"*Oh*!" Lloyd cried. "Damn, I know who it is now!"

"Because for you to sneak out on me after—"

"Tom, for gosh sakes! You know me better than that!"

"Does a guy ever know anyone but family, really?"

Lloyd stared at Tom. Then he said, "It was at Portia's. This realtor, who is a venomous little toad, started getting pushy with me at the pool party, and I fended him off. I stiffed him out, is what. So, for revenge, he's gone fibbing to Jake. Hoping to create trouble between you and me. And Jake, helpful as always, passes it all straight to you."

Tom turned the faucet back on, his features unreadable. "Wash," he ordered.

Lloyd cleaned a dish silently, while Tom thought it over.

Finally, Tom said, "So there's no underlying crime here? It's disinformation?"

"It's evil lies, and you should have known that as soon as you heard them!"

"Mad at me, huh?"

Lloyd took another dish, washing and fuming.

"I can't investigate in good faith?" Tom asked.

"There's nothing to investigate!"

"Well, that's why you look into the matter, to—"

"Tom, sometimes you are too rough with me."

"Hear about you wandering off to…got to punish you for your crimes, don't I? So my daddy did, and so will I."

"All right," said Lloyd, putting the plate down. "Now it's time, man, because you have caught me on just the right drink." Turning to look directly at Tom, Lloyd went on, "What kind of punishment was it, exactly? You tell me here and now."

Surprised at Lloyd's intensity, Tom hesitated. Then: "It was just and effective, angry though you are."

"Well, who *made* me angry?"

"Wash."

"*No.*"

"Rebellious as always. You know what I'll do about that."

"This again," Lloyd murmured.

"My daddy knew how to force rebellious kids to behave."

Lloyd turned off the faucet.

"Would he strike you?" Lloyd asked.

"Worse," Tom answered. That was all he would say.

In fact, Tom's father never hurt his children. When very young, they got sharp reprimands, or timeouts fiercely initiated: to frighten rather than to pain. As teens, they got stern and then sterner warnings. And if these didn't work, Tom's father would take the culprit in his arms and hold him until he felt ashamed by the might of such disappointed trust.

Winter blew in, as usual, from the Arctic and Canada, and Lloyd knew he ought to buy a heavy coat. He was short of funds, however, even now that Tom had lowered his rent to one dollar a month. Fearful of slipping into plastic debt, Lloyd tried to pretend that going around in his Ralph Lauren September-light Polo jacket was dashing.

Tom commented on it one Saturday morning over coffee, and Lloyd evaded the subject by asking what Tom was giving Lucy for her birthday.

"A meatball shaper," said Tom.

"What?"

"So she can make meatballs with your spaghetti recipe. And now, suddenly, the kids like it, too, though they get more spaghetti on their—"

"Tom, you cannot give your girl a meatball shaper for her birthday."

"Why the hell not?"

"Girls like emotional presents. Give her the shaper, sure. But on her birthday, you've got to address her heart."

Tom grinned. "Okay, professor. For instance?"

"Have you got a photograph? A nice one?"

"Got a tasty shot of old Jake in his running shorts," Tom replied, turning the newspaper over. "What a build on a guy, huh?"

"I meant of you and Lucy."

Tom sat there for a bit, then laughed outright. "Boy, you are easy," he said.

"Oh. I get it. Another of your crazy jokes. And I fell for it, so—"

"Yeah, but that's her present? A snapshot?"

"In a beautiful frame accompanied by poetry."

"Roses are red," Tom began, "violets—"

"No, Tom. You quote from, like, Byron or Keats. 'She walks in beauty like the night.'"

"Do what?"

Then Lloyd had an inspiration. "Why don't you fix her a frame? You must have all the makings in the tool bay. And we can pick up some poetry online."

Tom always did like making things in his father's old workshop, so the two of them pulled a photograph from Tom's souvenir box and took it into the garage, where Tom gathered materials like a high-school genius generating a science project. Metal. Glass. Cutting tools. "You like it plain or peanut?" Tom asked.

"Which means?"

"I can frame it in plain. Steady. Cool. You see this here? A sample." Tom showed Lloyd. "Or the gold. Fake but shiny."

"The genuine. Shiny stuff makes a great first impression, but it doesn't last."

Tom began then: measuring with a T-square, locking his subject in the vise, judging the cut.

"Gosh, Tom, you really know how this stuff goes."

Working away in his Irish fisherman's sweater, Tom said, "It's cold out here. Where's your sweater on?"

"Oh, I just..."

"You can wear one of mine."

"I have sweaters, Tom."

Tom put down the jigsaw and turned to Lloyd. "Go inside," he said, "and come back wearing one. Go along, now. You don't want me getting righteous on you."

When Lloyd came back, in a navy-blue V-neck, Tom was soldering the frame bottom to one of the sides.

"Lucy will love this, Tom. It's an honest-to-gosh love present."

"'To gosh'?" Tom echoed.

Lloyd shrugged. "Leftover orphanage stuff."

Watching Tom securing the glass and photo inside the now finished frame, Lloyd said, "With that expertise, I'm amazed you never did raise up your own model railroad."

Tom said nothing, so Lloyd went on. "We keep talking about doing it, but each time...because you...Still. We could just do it. Just start in and build a table in..." Careful, Lloyd. "In your dad's room. Now that the...door is open to it. You said so yourself."

For two minutes after that, Tom buffed the frame before saying, "What gauge would it be?"

"Absolutely HO."

"I'm almost done here. You...you want to go looking at the trains in The Hardware next?"

"I would *love* that, Tom. I would *love* to look at the trains with you."

Now Tom handed the framed photograph to Lloyd for inspection: Tom and Lucy happy at some street festival, his arm around her waist and the flicker of a smile at the pleasant absurdity of romance delighting her face.

The Hardware was jammed with Christmas crowd, especially in the area around the annual exhibition model railroad.

Tom didn't like what they had done with the opportunity. "There's no program to it," he said. "It's the whatever layout. An any-which-way world. Where's the real life in it? Authority. Questions about existence."

"I always wanted a trestle bridge," said Lloyd. "And even…now, don't laugh at me, okay?...an engineer's striped cap when I run the train."

Tom grinned.

There was another layout in the store, smaller and lacking audience. But when Tom investigated, he came back to Lloyd and pulled him by the arm to see it: a mountainous geography in which track hurtled around corners between some sort of arrogant industrial construction and an innocent, victimized little town.

Lloyd nodded. He liked it when Tom pulled him along by the arm, and when Tom analyzed the missions of the trains, and when folks in the store stared admiringly at Tom and wondered if he and Lloyd were related.

Another Saturday and more of The Game. Lucy and the kids were at Lucy's mother's, so it was just that horrible Jake, who came crashing into Lloyd's room with "I'm going to ball you like a chick, short stuff!"

"*Tom*!" cried Lloyd, at his desk, his eyes fixed on his computer screen.

From the living room, Tom amiably called out, "Leave my housemate alone, Jake!"

"When do we tell him?" Jake called back.

Lloyd waited till Tom appeared to ask him, "Tell me what?"

Jake answered. "Officer McThomas Buckner here made things hot for my realtor to even the score for, like, when he was blackening your fair name." To Tom, Jake added, "Except will that compromise the sale of my house?"

"Told you from the start to get another realtor, didn't I?"

"What happened, exactly?" Lloyd asked, turning around in his chair.

"That guy who started the rumor you were skipping out on your lease," Tom replied. "A true weasel."

"Just before you came," said Jake, "he tried to sell me his sister." Mock-solemn, Jake pulled off his cowboy hat and held it over his heart.

"What happened, Tom?" Lloyd asked again.

And again it was Jake who answered, as he put his Stetson back on his head: "My scumbag of a realtor was showing the house when Tom and I blew in. Very nice couple looking at it. Young marrieds from the Baptist church on Winneshiek. After all the screaming, they'll never look at houses again."

"When was this?"

"This morning," said Tom. "Helping Jake move his stuff out of the garage to the scrapyard, and we saw—"

"Officer McThomas offered to arrest my realtor, who began yelping a certain amount here and there all over my house."

"Arrest him for inventing those lies about me?"

asked Lloyd, closing down his laptop. "Accusing me of trying to sneak out on my lease?"

"Arrest him for he's a stupid irritating perv, how about?" said Tom.

"Which Officer McThomas proceeded to state at the time," Jake added. "*In* so many words, and I couldn't be happier."

"He tried to pretend that he didn't remember you," said Tom. "All a misunderstanding, as many a felon will say. Haven't I seen his act before, with deceitful eyes looking away as he double-talks me? Not to mention poking his fingers at me—physical provocation, designed to infuriate officers of the law. Very popular among that type."

Jake cut in with, "So Officer McThomas is, like, 'Oh, right, you don't remember?' A guy such as you does *not* remember a handsome fellow like the housemate here?" Looking at Lloyd, Jake added, "And in your cute shorts, too, right?"

"Jake—"

"Did you tell him that, Tom?"

Another of Tom's silences. It sounded odd in the room after the quick overturn of voices. Both Lloyd and Jake, used to Tom's momentary lulls, simply waited.

"He won't bother you again," said Tom at last. "I know that much."

Jake suddenly went very still, slowly turning around to end up looking right at Lloyd. Then he whispered, "Do you know what I'm going to do to you, little jazzboy?"

"You hold on there, Jake," said Tom.

Lloyd stood up, his eyes blazing, as Tom grabbed

Jake with "You going to miss the pre-game for me, now, Jake?"

"Let me smooch him up?"

"*Out*!" Tom cried, though he winked at Lloyd as he and Jake left.

Moving the laptop to one side, Lloyd sat back down, taking out a sheaf of the blank copy paper he had laid in. Now it begins: he made his first rough diagrams for the model railroad he and Tom would build. It would take many hours and a ton of sheets, but when Lloyd was sure of what he had he was going to make four-color plans to show Tom: a layout with fascinating towns, a mountain overlooking a trestle bridge, and perhaps a roundhouse for storing the rolling stock. Real life in it. Then they could start construction.

Tom was already on it, picking up four by eight plywood sheets, raw wood for joists and stringers, and two by fours from the lumber yard for the raising of the table. Sturdy. Permanent. Upon it, a little world would form and evolve as a simple starting oval reached out to branch lines and turnouts, as graded inclines accommodated the surrounding geography, as roads and figures socialized the space.

Tom and Lloyd worked on their table only when both were free at the same time, because it was theirs to create together; if either was to sneak in and advance the project by himself, it would have felt like adultery. Tom set up a miniature tool bay there, where his father had lived and died, with an X-Acto knife folded into a safety case, needle-nose pliers, a screwdriver set, tweezers, a rail nipper, a mill file and needle files, pastels and dull cote for weathering, paints and brushes, and a variety of adhesives for work with plastic, metal, or wood.

"Aviator glasses?" asked Lloyd, rummaging around in the shallow see-through plastic tray while Tom worked on the table.

"When you cut rail," said Tom, aligning one table leg with a corner of the top, "little bits of metal go crashing right up at you."

Striking a pose in the glasses, Lloyd said, "'Men, this mission we fly today will save a corrupt and unknowing world!'"

"How about you fetch me the hammer which I can't reach it while holding all this together, instead of playacting the day away?"

Handing over the hammer, Lloyd said, "'Commander, the men are proud to serve under you.'" Tom suppressed a smile as Lloyd added, "'They're too shy to tell you themselves, sir.'"

"How about giving me a little room, Lindbergh?"

"Boy, you really could have started this thing anytime, Tom. You always had it in mind, right? Why did you wait till now?"

Working a nail a half-inch into the wood before he hammered it, Tom said, "I sent for the Walther's catalogue. From Wisconsin." After hammering a bit, he put in, "Because they won't have everything we need in The Hardware. We can make a start, sure. First purchase is always a locomotive, right? Track and a bit of stock. Gravel, tree stuff. Maybe a house or two. Get the feel of the thing as it begins."

"Gosh, there's so much…makingness in it. I

guess that's why guys get so proud of their layouts."

"Didn't you do any building on that railroad at the orphanage?"

"It was all built when we got it. The family came over and set it up for us. The Hickses, by name. Then they shook hands with us, and we just started running it."

Tom readied another nail in the wood. "Shook hands with you?"

"Yes. Even the youngest kids in the family. It was very ceremonial, and they said 'Good morning' while they did it. Sister Charity lined us up for it, and I liked it so much that I got back on line so I could shake hands again."

Tom hammered the nail home.

"Later on, we'd ask if we could add some buildings to the layout, but Sister said that would be ungrateful."

Tom leaned the table top along the wall and turned to Lloyd with the grin he wore when he teased. "Sister Charity, was it? Wonder if you boys ever jacked off to a thought of Sister Charity when she wasn't solving problems like Maria."

"That would be blasphemy eight times over."

Tousling Lloyd's hair, Tom said, "Let's get this place cleaned up, now."

"What about the towns, Tom?" Lloyd asked, as they put the room to rights. "Plastic models or build our own?"

Collecting the tools and nesting them in the bay, Tom offered, "That start-from-scratch hobbycrafting stuff never really works. Everything ends up looking like a cake decoration. I'd stick with the kits. The

Walther's book will give us a fine selection. Maybe we'll rip a few of them up and put them together in our own way, if you so desire. Personalize it, you know."

"Boy. We could start any day, right?"

"Soon as we get this table up and you take off those dopey glasses."

After law enforcement and the gym, Tom gave most of his time to Lucy, and weekends were official Tom Days for the kids. Still, Tom and Lloyd stole stray hours out of Tom's schedule, and, as winter set in, the table was all but finished. Tom continued to observe that Lloyd roamed about town in a coat meant for autumn. Lloyd replied that he didn't do all that much roaming.

"Rebellious as ever" was Tom's assessment.

But at least all of Lloyd's places were nearby. His relationship with the newspaper was conducted online, and his gym and shopping lay in the mall across the road. The only real jaunt in Lloyd's routine was his bike ride to the pool party. And, as it happened, Lloyd hadn't been attending much lately.

In fact, Lloyd hadn't been going at all. Then—greatly to his surprise—Junior made one of those "Hello, stranger" phone calls.

"Everybody's asking for you," Junior told him. "Clark says you've found a racier crowd. You know how he likes to speculate. Who could they be, Lloyd?"

"The crowd I found isn't racy."

"So there *is* another set! Will you write your newspaper columns about them now? We've got new slang for you, though. When Clark really freaks for something, he says, 'That is so *distributed.*' I use it, too."

Lloyd missed them. He remembered wryly, fondly, how Junior would rush over when Clark launched some new bit of mischief to join in on it, or how the servants would go professionally blind when Clark announced "The Las Vegas Pas de Deux Contest" and dared one of the girls to take part. And Lloyd missed the hyper food presentations and swimming in the heated water and he missed Portia.

But showing hunger is the first sin, and Lloyd carefully doesn't mention Portia to Junior. He waits Junior out, because Lloyd is certain this call is an assignment. And as anyone can tell you, it isn't Clark or Annamarie who gives the orders in that group.

And yet. They kept on talking without Junior's ever quite getting to Portia. He had no message from her to Lloyd—no she wants to see you again or is so sorry for fixing a low rating on you or dismissing you with that ray gun of the haveitall young.

No, Junior sailed right along to "You'll come tonight, won't you? I know you will, guy, with those smart grownup's jokes of yours, and your manly charm."

Doesn't anybody work around here besides the servants? Lloyd wondered, as they took his things. It isn't vacationland any more. Summer is over. It's time to begin. But those kids were still foofing around. Lloyd tried to picture growing up with them at St. Catherine's, imagining how they would suit the havenothing culture of thrown-away children living on a state budget. No—here she is: Portia. It costs money to smile to like that, Lloyd thought, as she came toward him.

"My lovely Lloyd," she said. "You've been writing about such incongruous things of late. The etiquette for watching television football. Shoppers at the Hardware. And model trains!"

She gently waved a no-no finger at him, then took his hand and kissed it.

"Hello, Portia."

She looked very right. Not…sumptuous, no, but sweet and able. If I were Clark, she'd say yes in a second, wouldn't she?

Annamarie and Junior crowded around, welcoming Lloyd with more than casual warmth, he thought. And Clark paid him the ultimate compliment, guiding Lloyd's hands to Clark's upper arm to feel the separations.

"See how nice?" Clark asked him, and of course Junior cut in with "Try mine!"

Lloyd was looking at Portia.

"They're children," she told him, with such appeal, such guiltless beauty. "You can tell them anything, and they'll believe. You can take them anywhere, and they'll have fun."

Lloyd had carefully planned his speech; now he forgot the words. He drew her away from the others. He said, "I've missed you."

"Yes. More."

"You hurt me that time, you know."

"But it's so easy to do," she said, regretfully. She touched his arm.

"Do that to me," said Junior, who had come up

behind them.

"The new F. Scott Fitzgerald," Portia said, of Lloyd. "Explaining golden youth to America."

"I'm a golden youth," said Junior.

They swam relay races, Portia choosing Lloyd as her partner against Clark and Annamarie. Junior was the referee, and even before they started he cried, "Clark is the winner!"

The supper was a taco smorgasbord, with individual ingredients set out so each diner could invent a unique dish. (Clark skipped the taco and gorged on steak and mushrooms neat.) The conversation was heady: *True Blood*, the poor game support for the Nintendo 3DS, the pointlessness of hats. Lloyd hadn't remembered these kids being even that lively. And Portia haunted him like a fiancée, skinning him with her hands as if she really liked him.

I enjoy myself too much here, Lloyd was thinking. They make it so easy to be around them, and if your attention wanders they turn seductive, tempting. This whole loop is made of sin.

"You always go too soon," Portia complained; she could tell he was about to leave. "The chauffeur can drive you later."

"What time is it?" Lloyd asked. He had given his watch to Junior before the relays.

"You've still got all this time left," said Clark.

"No, I probably don't," Lloyd answered. "And I need to be prompt."

Portia said, "Come for a talk," and in the changing room, alone with Lloyd, she wove a tapestry of wishes. "But you know Daddy," she said, several times. She sighed a lot. "And Clark is such a zany idiot, really." Lloyd was normally a good listener, but Portia was like a contestant in a beauty pageant who wants a raise in her credit max instead of world peace. One tunes out. Lloyd kept hoping that Portia would initiate a sexual encounter—it was unwritten law that the girls made the first move—but Annamarie kept bustling in. Once Junior opened the door, said, "I'm drunk, Lloyd, are you?" and immediately vanished.

"It's all so endless," Portia was saying.

Lloyd got to his feet. He suddenly realized that he had had one glass too many. "Where's the chauffeur, then?" he asked. "And Junior has my watch."

Lloyd went out to the pool, where Annamarie and the two boys were performing a water ballet. Lloyd kept trying to get Junior's attention, and finally he leaped into the water, accosted Junior, and demanded his watch.

"It's over there, sweetheart," said Junior, gesturing as vaguely as possible.

While Lloyd hunted for it, Portia hovered about. Once she giggled.

"It's not funny," Lloyd murmured. Then, turning back to the pool, from which Junior was just emerging, he said, "Junior, will you *please* tell me where my watch is?"

"Right in the middle of such an intimate talk, though," said Portia. "Really, Lloyd."

"It's just a watch, dude," said Junior, joining them as he toweled off. "And what's so intimate? Does this mean you two are going to get engaged now?" Junior asked.

"Oh, I don't think so," Clark put in as he came up.

"Damn, who is *that* guy?" said Junior, staring over Lloyd's shoulder.

The other kids looked, too, while Lloyd got almost frantic in his hunting. "Will somebody for gosh sake please help me find—"

"Is that your brother, dude?" Clark asked Lloyd, turning him around to see:

Tom, in his sleeveless down coat, flannel shirt, corduroys, and snow boots, his eyes dialed to lock and load.

"You have one exact minute to get dressed," Tom told Lloyd. "After sixty, I'll drag you out of here naked as a jay if it comes to that."

Stunned for three seconds, Lloyd then broke for the changing room, pulling his pants on over his wet trunks and grabbing for his shirt as Portia and Annamarie ran in.

"That *is* your brother!" cried Portia.

"I want to fuck him!" said Annamarie.

"Find my shoes for heaven's sake!"

"He's everything!" Portia noted.

"And so much more," Annamarie agreed.

Handing Lloyd a right shoe (Clark's, but Lloyd put it on, anyway), Portia observed, "There's nothing like king size, is there?"

In the pool area, Clark and Junior were keeping Tom busy. Clark asked to feel Tom's biceps, and Tom snarled back, "How about you do some good in the world and tell that son-of-a-bitch to step on it?"

"Better step on it, Lloyd," Clark lazily called out.

"I've got bigger deltoids than Clark," Junior told Tom.

With his shirt only half-buttoned (unevenly at

that) and his belt missing, wearing one of Clark's and one of Junior's shoes, and still watchless, Lloyd came running out while struggling into his jacket. Portia and Annamarie followed him, and Portia it was who spotted the missing watch, so close to the taco platter that it was half-hidden under the lip of the plate.

"Oh, here it is, Lloyd," Portia called out. As she moved to bring it to him, Tom suddenly stepped forth, went up to her, and held out his hand for it.

"He has no right to that," said Tom, shoving it into his pocket. The four kids turned to look at Lloyd and see how he took this puzzling yet arresting development, but his face was blank, and he stood motionless till Tom marched up to him, grabbed his arm, and took him away with a "Good night, all."

The door slammed shut, and Junior said, "Bash me, did you *see* that guy?"

"Are they really brothers?" asked Annamarie. "They don't look alike."

"At all," Portia added. "And yet…"

"That was a genuine older-brother scowl on the big guy's face, though," Clark observed. "I bet Lloyd's going to get it tonight. He's going dark, wait and see."

"As long as there are guardians, there's going to be rules," said Junior. "It was bound to happen."

In the car, Lloyd sensed that trying to talk to Tom would only antagonize him more; they rode back in silence. When they docked and both got out, Tom said only, "Move!" Inside, he reset the safety alarm, turned to Lloyd, and ordered him to follow Tom to his room.

When they got there, Tom sat Lloyd on the bed

and, towering over him, said, “Can you give me one reason not to beat the tar out of you tonight?”

A couple of answers occurred to Lloyd—light ones, not flip but soothing—yet in the end he just said, “Can I take off my coat?”

Ignoring that, Tom said, “You know how strict I am about the house curfew. Which is midnight. Not”—as he checked his watch—“almost one-thirty A.M. by now.”

Lloyd got up to get his coat off, but Tom told him to sit back down.

“I wouldn’t put this man’s anger to the test if I were you,” Tom told him.

Lloyd sat.

“Jake warned me to give you a licking right off. Then you’d behave because you’d know what to be afraid of.”

“I know what to be afraid of, Tom.”

“No, you *should* be afraid of being rebellious!”

Disloyal! Irresponsible!

“Tom, I know I should have phoned up to say…and so on, but I lost my watch. The time just…and I must have had too much to drink, which isn’t like me at all. I feel a little lightheaded.”

“Lightheaded? That’s what you feel? *Lightheaded*?”

“‘He shall be slain immediately upon the place,’” Lloyd quoted. “Yes, because they smooched me up, and I let them. They took me out of myself with…the sweet temptation of security…”

Lloyd stopped speaking as Tom angrily took off his own coat and gloves and threw them onto his desk without taking his eyes off Lloyd. The gloves landed on the desktop next to a book Lloyd had not seen before, but before he could focus on it Tom was on his case.

"You know what you're about to feel instead of lightheaded?" Tom asked Lloyd.

"But if I had called to say I would be late just this special night, I might have awakened you."

"I don't go to bed until you're home, and you know that!"

"That's right, Tom. Checking up on me, to see if I'm obedient."

"To see if you're *safe* here and out of the possibility of *harm*!"

Lloyd went silent.

Pursuing his text, Tom asked, "And there you are, playing around with rich kids! Lost your watch, huh? And still running around in that cheap playtime coat when I—"

"*Tom*! Is that…on the desk, is that the Walther's catalogue?"

Now Lloyd jumped up. Tom grabbed him by the shoulders to push him back down, but Lloyd held his ground, trying to break away to get to the desk. "It came today, didn't it? Why didn't you tell me right off?"

Tom forced Lloyd back onto the bed, Lloyd holding Tom's arms, trying to relieve the pressure and stand on his own.

"How was I supposed to know that it arrived today?" Lloyd cried. "Yes, and *that's* why you're so sore at me! Because you think I skipped out on our first…because I don't care about the trains, right? I betrayed you? You think I would flip you off for those…those goodtime chuckleheads? Those toy people? Well, I have so spat with the whole gang—you see if I haven't! It's back to Avatar with the lot of them!"

Confused for a moment, Tom relaxed his grip, allowing Lloyd to dart off to his room. Soon enough, Tom followed in an insultingly confident amble.

"I don't know where you think you're going" came Tom's voice down the hall, nearing Lloyd's bedroom. "But when I get my hands on you, you will not be happy tonight."

Pulling open the top drawer of his desk, Lloyd got out a manila folder just as Tom entered, moving right up to Lloyd to force him backward by sheer presence.

Now pressed against the wall, Lloyd said, quite calmly, "You're not going to hurt me, Tom, and we both know that."

With an angry "I'll hurt you if I want to," Tom set his hands on Lloyd's shoulders as if to fix him in place, but Lloyd managed to raise the folder into view between them.

"Look at this, Tom."

"Why should I?"

They stood there for a while, Tom holding Lloyd and blazing at him. Then he let go of Lloyd and took the folder from him, never moving his eyes off Lloyd's.

"What's in it?" said Tom.

Lloyd didn't answer.

"You going to tell me or not?" Tom went on, as Lloyd's left hand felt his right shoulder where Tom had pressed it.

"Tom, just…just look at it, will you?"

Tom flipped the folder open, glanced at its contents, looked back at Lloyd. Then he went over to Lloyd's desk and spread open the four sheets of paper that he had found in the folder: Lloyd's schematics of their model railroad. Not the roughs, but fair copies painstakingly executed in four-color draftsmanship, using the tools in the garage.

"Here's the layout, I see," said Tom, after a long while, staring down at the drawings. "The serious town and the crazy town." The Tom and the Lloyd of it. "And this?"

Joining Tom at the desk, Lloyd said, "Yes, that's the trestle bridge I told you about. I measured the elevation in inches and it…see, it rises from the southeast on a trunk line and tunnels through the mountain…here…to join the main line in the northwest. See how the bridge runs directly over another line, northeast to southwest?"

Looking at one of the town plans, Tom noted, "Bank. Grocery. Wait…a bike rental?"

"Well, it's small. To save space."

"Took time to do all this, I bet."

Opening one of the desk drawers, Lloyd hauled out a stack of roughs nearly an inch high. Tom had a look at them, too, comparing them to the fair copies, nodding here and there and grunting once in agreement with something or other.

"Tom feels betrayed by his buddy," said Lloyd, "only to discover that he has actually been extravagantly reaffirmed."

Now Tom was inspecting the town and bridge plans next to the full layout plan, noting where tiny details in the main blueprint enjoyed specifications in the smaller ones, coded to size and material through orange and brown ink.

"It isn't fun when anyone is mad at you," said Lloyd. "But when I'm getting madded at by such a handsome guy, it's really hard to bear."

Tom looked at Lloyd. "What's handsome got to do with it, for hell sakes?"

"Everything."

Tom dug into a pocket of his trousers.

"Here," he said, handing Lloyd his watch back.

"Boy, I'll be hearing plenty about you tomorrow from the guys," said Lloyd, fastening his watch on his left wrist. "I mean, if I give them access."

Still immersed in the plan for the crazy town, Tom nevertheless asked, "You think the blonde liked me? You know the one I mean."

"That's Annamarie. She wants to fuck you."

Tom looked up. "She said that? Those words?"

"The young talk that way now."

"Yeah? I'm young, and I don't—"

"Well, the rich young. It's the latest cool."

"She better not talk that way around me."

Putting the four plans back into the folder, Tom said, "Guess you can take off that coat now, which I would love not to see it again till Second Coming."

Lloyd left his coat on his bed, and the two men went back through the house to Tom's room. When they got there, Tom laid the folder carefully atop the Walther's catalogue. Then he and Lloyd took an over-the-sink washup and a tooth-brushing in the bathroom. Back in the bedroom, Tom poured water from his night jug into the glass and, as Lloyd came up to him, handed him the glass.

"Drink half," Tom said. "You got your watch back for okayness and now some water, which is to smooth you down from trouble."

Lloyd was thirsty, in fact. He drank half the glass and gave it to Tom, who finished it off. Then Tom said, "Understand me now, you have to be punished for your crimes or there'll never be peace between us."

"I know a really terrifying punishment," said Lloyd. "You could tell me all is forgiven and we won't mention it again."

"The hell kind of punishment is that?"

Lloyd shrugged. "I thought it was worth a shot."

"Hop into bed, now. And don't let me catch you with a resistful look."

On the contrary, Lloyd would probably have on something approaching his third smile, a thin line lightly wrinkled by a touch of that-was-close relief. The two undressed and went under the covers, and now Tom spoke:

"It's like that day I caught you crying, isn't it? Poor little thirty-six-year-old orphan, and he's all out there with rich nobodies learning the arts of goofing off. Classic guy, right? But he can't get a break, nobody to make sure that he's home safe, care about him and such. Serving his apples-and-cheese combo to an ungrateful diner. Little boy wakes up in the huge darkness, and he's scared, so he crawls into bed with his soldier dad, and you think I don't know about that, don't you? How that little boy feels. Well, sir, first thing tomorrow we'll have one of those breakfasts you sometimes make, with all the trimmings. Eggs and biscuits. Juice fresh squoze. Bacon, coffee with special heated milk. Next I'll take you to Shepherd's and buy you a coat and scarf, so that's settled about getting you warm for the winter. Then we'll go to The Hardware and look at the trains. Make our first buy. Yeah, a transformer, and I already know which locomotive. We'll take the Walther's along, decide on stock. A few building models, too, keep us busy. But no rushing into it. We'll make copies of your draw plans, take them along. Orderly. Long-range. Get it all home, start our layout, first day. That table is waiting for us, isn't it? Sure. Then I want to take you out to dinner. One of those steak places where you get your potato baked in its individual foil just for you. Sour cream on it, classic. And then I'll drive you back here and punish you for your crimes, because we're going deep, us two. Believe I knew just what to do from the moment you came into my house that day. And you knew what was in store, right? Tuck you in, now, so we can both sleep easy. Blanket goes up to the ear and no farther, because that's how my daddy used to do it. Catch on to it? You close your eyes now, Lloyd boy. We've got a big day tomorrow, and Tom is right here by your side."

HOPELESSLY DEVOTED TO YOU

JASON:

Well! The queens are still debating *just* when it all began—when our little jewel of Luzerne County in the Commonwealth of Pennsylvania first stirred with the realization that we had been

Chosen!

For!

Immortality!

There are those who will try to tell you that it started with the opening of our very own gay bar, Mahantango Mary's. Some called it posh, some poison—but to me and my friends it was a personal clubhouse loaded for a permanent Anything Can Happen Day. You oh so fashionable gays of the two coasts may be surprised to learn that we of flyover America have our chic drop-in salon, where the near-great meet the great to chin and gin.

Or it *might* have started when Mahantango Mary's opened. It might have. But most of us will date the start of the action from the moment when Lyle Hickock, automobile mechanic to the stars and the hottest man in town, suddenly got that look in his eye and set off a-cruising for something steady in the romantic line.

Lyle Hickock. How to describe him, now...*yes*! You know the dreamy, thoughtful, poetic sort of beau? Well, that's not Lyle. No, Lyle is lean, hung, and dangerous. Excuse me, *allegedly*! No one really knows *what* Lyle is, because he likes to date around in foreign parts, such as Wilkes-Barre, or even Reading. Well, that is...he *used* to date around, before he met—but I'm getting ahead of the story. Let me put it this way: *at this time* Lyle favored the one-night stand or the lost weekend (allegedly), but every so often he yearned for something lasting and local. And that is when Lyle made his debut at—as we took to calling it—Mary's.

Of course, that prancing dynamo Alistair Tessier was the first among our set to spot Lyle, who can be unassuming when he wants to be. Alistair had been trying to chat up a Wilkes College English professor who *clearly* found Alistair entirely too fizzy for his academic taste. (*Well*!) And that was when Alistair caught sight of Lyle, *right there in the bar*! So he gave up on the professor and came running over to us to lurk about in his smug Alistair way. Because he wasn't going to waste his dish until *everybody* was listening. And when we had all presented him with an expectant silence, Alistair *finally* whispered, "Legend in the making, girls—Lyle Hickock has just walked in!"

"*No*!" we cried, to the last man.

"Yes," he averred. "The saga has found its hero."

And some do indeed claim that it all started that evening. Lyle's First Night, you might say. But Lyle had to make more than one foray into Mary's before he found what he liked. Those "I'm so *woof* they're changing the word sex to my name" types can be v-e-r-y selective.

So I know better, and now it can be told: everything *really* began when our very own porn star came to town. *Yes*—the wonderful Jutter Flexx, famed in song and story, so special yet so basic *and* so masculine yet so impish, turned up out of nowhere, bartending in Mary's. And, let me say: the *queens* were *flabbergasted*!

Now, this was *before* Lyle Hickock started coming in. So we of course presumed that, sooner or later, Jutter would hook up with Mary's resident hunk, Todd Rifflin. You'll know his type—one of those blond teases who says, "My straight friends think I'm gay and my gay friends think I'm straight." Except he doesn't have any straight friends. (But I digress.) Of course, everyone tells Todd he should just zoom off to Cal and star for the Falcon Studio. I mean, doesn't he have the *look*! But perhaps he prefers the "big fish, small pond" lifestyle. Some do, you know. They fear the competition of the gala places, where coming around the corner is someone as cute as you with two extra inches.

At that, Mary's was filled with…well, not hunks, no. But what I like to call Personality Stars. *Yes*! Such as Phil Conroy, the wickedest queen alive! But never mind all that, because—without a *shred* of warning—there among us was the new Mary's bartender…Jutter

Flexx in person!

And may I say? Jutter looked even better than in his pictures, with a toothy smile and an easy, affable nod when he took your drink order. He didn't dress to show off, as you might have expected—just striped T-shirts and usual jeans. No muscle tops or denim gone wild. But then, here was a boy who could show off just by showing up. He was pure poster—the modernized clone, with his famous hairy chest and snazzy mustache, and the sleek muscles instead of the Superman measurements. Jutter seemed rather like the guy you might run into in the super-drug, allowing just a minute of friendly chat before he moved on with his life and left you amazed in the aisles. What I call hot but friendly.

And were the *queens* in a *state*! Phil Conroy's At Homes were *completely* given over to discussions on how best to approach Jutter—because there he was, night after night, our new Mary's bartender, pouring drinks and utterly garnishing away with those lemon doodads and chirping out thrilling little thank yous for his tips. Of course we splurged—who wouldn't, to get a load of that smile? And yet. Why was he *here*, of all places? He had no local family that any of us knew of. And believe a queen—we would know!

There were those who reasoned that he must be pumped full of Attitude. You know—that "I've had sex in Cal and you haven't" thing. But if you make assumptions about a guy and snipe at him…well, isn't he going to snipe right back? Alistair Tessier grumped at Jutter because—so Alistair claimed—there was a peculiar savor in his Heidi Crush on the rocks. And of course one thing led to another, as it always does with

Alistair. And finally the bar manager had to warn him that he was on his way to losing his customer rights in Mary's.

Phil Conroy, now—Phil said, "Just wait till Todd Rifflin makes his move." Whatever that meant. Because who could guess what move Todd might make, multisexual curiosity that he is? Still, beauty does follow beauty. And in due course Todd made his entrance into Mary's, and Todd scoped Jutter and Jutter scoped Todd. Then they did the flirt thing under the cover of "just a pair of cool straight boys talking." Although, now that I mention it, nobody knew for sure if Jutter was a cousin or gay for pay.

Anyway, I didn't get all that involved in the Jutter Flexx Story just yet, because my best friend, Rick, had suddenly abandoned Manhattan and come to live in our town. How he and I got separated is a long story, and I'll tell it some time—but when he was asked why he left New York, Rick would reply, "To look up a long-lost friend."

Isn't that sweet?

RICK:

Okay. In the first place, Jutter Flexx was not a porn star. He had done some modeling for Colt, and he did become one of their most exploited figures, with his own solo calendar. In the gay world, this is like being elected President of France. Still, Jutter Flexx never appeared in a video with a partner; I don't believe he ever even soloed.

This gave him a unique place in the hierarchy,

because unlike the other visual icons of the day, like Ken Ryker or Matthew Rush, Jutter had revealed nothing but his skin and his smile. Part of his attraction was that he was, however famous, absolutely uncollected—mysterious and intimate at once.

And he stayed that way, tending bar at Mahantango Mary's with an impenetrable amiability. Of course he struck up a mild acquaintance with Todd Rifflin. It was an alliance based on mutual self-defense, for Todd, too, had a lot to protect from nosy parkers, and much of the nightly "drama" in the bar consisted of various people trying to filch secrets out of various other people.

My pal Jason, I'm glad to report, did not indulge in this "hotrodding," as he and his gang term it. Jason has a sense of honor and even a respect for other people's privacy. It's unusual in a...well, yes. A queen.

Do you have a least favorite saying? Mine is "There's someone I'd like you to meet." As in: you're in some social situation, a party or whatever, deep in conversation with someone. Maybe a buddy, maybe someone new and pleasant. Suddenly, some jerk who simply will not leave anything be comes butting in to introduce some stranger, wasting everybody's time as the two of you then have to improvise cocktail-party fill.

What I ask is, *why* is there someone he'd like me to meet? Is it an eccentric millionaire who gives away fortunes at parties? Is it Hugh Jackman? Isn't it, in fact, just a guy he's using in order to puppet the rest of us around, which for some reason makes him feel important?

That's been on my mind for a while, because ever since I came here I've been getting that introduction stuff to a painful degree. I once went so far as to ask one of these numbskulls just why he felt the need to interfere with my evening. In just those words. He looked at me as if I'd addressed him in Hindustani.

I was also getting a lot of my second least favorite saying, "I've heard so much about you." Inevitable, no? Jason and I were best friends, after all, and when you're that close to a gay man he tends to bring you up a lot. Like straight men always mentioning their wives. It's that "other half" of you, the being who affirms or confutes your existence. Jason had pridefully told his circle my line about "looking up a long-lost friend," so of course they immediately assumed that was just some pretext. One by one, privately—or as privately as possible in this coterie where everyone minds everyone else's business—they asked me why I *really* left New York. I gave them each a different story. To Phil Conroy, the most self-important of the gang, I explained that once I hit thirty-five I couldn't take the pressure to stay cute and built.

"And Jason had told me," I said, at I hoped my most ingratiating, "how much easier it is to be gay in a small town."

"Oh, I wouldn't call it 'easy,'" Phil replied. "I'd call it…'select.'"

"Of course," I agreed. "That's just the word."

"Mmm, yes. But don't butter me up, sweetheart. I'm not a croissant."

I was more successful with Alistair Tessier, the most demanding of the group if he lacked attention but the most amenable if you paid some. I fed him a complex fiction about the horrors of keeping matchmakers at bay.

"Manhattan," said I, "is populated almost exclusively by women with unmarried girl friends."

"The *horror*!" he cried. "But don't they know you're gay?"

"To unmarried women and their allies, there is no such thing as gay or straight. There are only two types of male: husbands and human sacrifices. As I am unmarried, I belong to the latter." Drawing him close for a confidence, I whispered, "If I dropped my guard for even a moment, I would be ensnared by a bridezilla."

"They're *everywhere*!" he put in, clearly thrilled that I was trusting him with personal material. "No beauty is safe!"

"Beauty?" I echoed. "Once she's over thirty, the New York bachelorette would take Dracula's cousin Zoltan."

In fact, I left New York because I was bored with it. I had collected New York like a matchbook: where to eat, how to dress, whom to quote. I needed to be uninformed once again, young and bewildered. I wanted my wonder back.

The real question is: Why did Jutter Flexx come to town? What was he looking for in one of the least imposing cities in all Luzerne County?

JASON:

Well! Didn't the Jutter stories keep coming? His

parents live nearby, a wealthy admirer was setting him up in a passion cottage for two, he was returning to college on a local scholarship. Phil Conroy's At Homes were *consumed* with speculation! But we should cut to the romance, so let me speak—*finally*!—of the night Jutter Flexx met Lyle Hickock.

First, the boilerplate. Lyle really *was* the town mechanic, as surely as if he had been elected to the post, like a mayor. He ran his own business, a fixit garage called Hickock Motors, and anyone with a brain and a troubled auto sent it to Lyle's shop. He charged top fee, but he could repair anything and never cheated with hidden add-ons. Other garages would flub jobs or expand them falsely. Lyle was honest.

That's the boring part. I mean, cars? *Please*. What matters is that Lyle was the maddest tall masculine underspoken big hands scavenging eyes chin of death not exactly handsome but *cannot* take your eyes off him character in the province. Queens would go ever so silent around him, or simply cascade to the floor in an opera trill of despair.

And the *stories*! He was brutal, he was tender, he was twins, he was a hit man. They said that if a boy friend displeased him, Lyle would take him into a private room in the garage, force boxing gear on him, and punch him around to a tape of crowd noises at a championship fight.

He'd say, "We'll just put on the gloves and go a few rounds, buddy boy." Allegedly. And I can only add that Lyle would have looked utterly devastating in those dippy oversized boxer's shorts they have—you know, where the waist is too high? Everlast, like love eternal. Except Lyle's love was Blitzkrieg.

Only his ex-boy friends could tell for certain, true. But no one knew any of Lyle's ex-boy friends. They were the invisible man.

"*Precisely*," said Alistair Tessier, whatever that's supposed to mean.

"The grisly tales!" Phil Conroy put in.

Kenny Fox made remark: "Lyle Hickock has the shoulders of a *murderer*!"

"And," Phil Conroy purred. "Don't they say that the City Council has been bribed?"

"To do what?" Alistair asked.

And Kenny, helping himself to his fourth pink lady (a regional favorite, lemon cupcakes with cherry-apple icing), put in "Doesn't Lyle fix their cars for free?"

Sex, corruption, secrets…these are a few of our favorite things. But then came the night—at *last*!—when Lyle showed up in Mary's while Jutter was tending bar. Lyle stood around for a bit as the chatter level in the whole place rose from 3 to 9. Waiting just enough time for Jutter to take a few good looks and think it over, Lyle then went up to him and ordered a beer. What *brand*, you ask? The brand was *Love Me Tonight*!

"Their eyes crashed like *cymbals*!" Phil Conroy ever recalled.

"Jutter was *helpless*!" Kenny Fox added.

"And Lyle smiled his pickpocket's smile and said, 'I haven't seen you here before. Do you live with your folks?'" Phil's version.

"No, he said, 'You ever box, handsome?'" Kenny.

"Actually, what he said was 'My truck's outside. Can I give you a lift somewhere?'"

That was me. And they all stopped. They put down their cakes and coffees and waited. In their soul of souls, as true and righteous queens, they knew what Jutter's answer to that must be.

RICK:

I have to admit, Lyle Hickock did give our boy Jutter pause. In his California period as a prominent model, Jutter no doubt had crossed paths with many a professional hunk. And I would guess that he got any one of them he wanted.

Nevertheless, Lyle was what you don't see all that much of in the modeling world: natural, break-the-rules sexy. His muscles came from labor rather than the gym, and his style was accidental. Lyle never entered a room: he just walked in. And he didn't strike some studied pose: he waited, simply standing there. If he liked you, he went over to you. And if you liked him back, he took you home.

Anyway, all of Mary's was avidly watching Lyle and Jutter talking over the bar. When other customers came up, Jutter would wave them off to the other bartender on duty, without taking his eyes off Lyle. He was on love break, I guess. No one had ever seen Jutter focus on anyone like this, and small towns do enjoy their little dramas. A straight crowd would have started calling out bets on whether or not Lyle would get Jutter home that night; gambling is one of the things hetero males are genetically inclined to, like playing basketball or jumping bail. Mary's clientele simply turned into that thing that homo males are born to be: an audience. At the theatre, at an Oscar night soirée, or just innocently bystanding as Joan Rivers and Arianna Huffington dispute rights to the last remaining unit at a Hollywood gift-bag table, gays know how to appreciate the arts. Why? Because we're so good at performing ourselves.

Around straights.

No, I'm slipping off-topic. The time: late. The place: Lyle meets Jutter at Mary's. The boys: one grinning masculine youth and one mysteriously threatening slightly older guy. Lyle was mysterious not because of any slithery attitudes, but because he was so seldom seen around town. His customers at Hickock Motors never spoke to or even glimpsed Lyle. All they got was Miss McEwen, the young woman at the front desk. Legally, she had just become Mrs. Raimondi, but she continued as Miss McEwen because that better described her business manner, which was concise and unyielding. Short to the edge of the brusque: *Miss*. Pointed and fast-moving, no waster of time: *McEwen*. It was she who passed on to you the details of the repair assessment and warned you what the bill would run to, and if you were foolish enough to resent any part of it—or even ask a passing but unnecessary question or two—she would fix you with a look and say, "We have a policy, sir." Worse, if you asked to speak to Mr. Hickock himself, perhaps out of a sense of self-importance, Miss McEwen would allow only that one of the mechanics might be available at some future time, "schedule permitting." She would affect a dubious tone for the last bit, because We have a policy, sir. And if, after this mildly encoded warning to back off, you persisted, you would be given the contact information for other garages in the area. That meant that you were more or less banned from Hickock Motors.

So even Lyle's regular customers had never met him, and that gives rise to legends. False ones. The business about Lyle's boxing sessions, for instance: he did enjoy sparring for a round or two, but not with an unwilling partner. Once you agreed, however, Lyle did like it edgy. He never spoke of "having sex," much less of "making love." He'd say, "I want to work you over." And I can tell you this for fact: when one of Lyle's dates asked why he got so intense when fucking, Lyle would shrug and say, "It's just something that's in me."

As for the tales of Lyle's being down with the city fathers: the guy who owns the go-to garage is down with everyone who matters. This is taking us very far from the beating heart of our Luzerne County Romance, but I want to take us yet farther and do a bit about the town and what it was like to move in, total stranger, with one very close friend to squire me around.

I need to do this, because some metropolitan gays nourish preconceptions about small-town gay life. They think the cuisine consists of your mother's tin of index cards from the 1960s, the clothes are Look what I found in the attic, and the sex is hayseeds coming too soon.

In fact, cities have the museums, theatres, and restaurants, but otherwise gay culture is the same all over America. That's why newbies fit in so easily.

Jason made it even easier for me, because—as we have seen—he belonged to a set. What gay guy doesn't? Has there ever been a lonesome queen? Unhappy, perhaps. Even loveless and frustrated. But never lonesome: we live like wolves, in packs.

Jason's pack leader was Phil Conroy, the one who gave all the major At Homes. Phil had the nicest place, and he was a generous host. Not that the queens needed a lot of refreshment: they dined on fun. They were really quite friendly to me after a prelude of being suspicious, if only as a formality. Jason said they favored me because he had warned them to treat me with respect. But I think they genuinely enjoyed having someone new to try their old routines on.

Phil's act was the most venerable, tweaked and rejuvenated over the years—*The Bette Davis Show*, a television variety hour in the now defunct format of hostessed song, dance, and sketch comedy. Like what Carol Burnett used to do. Phil played Bette, miming the cigarette in his right hand as he tried to discourage the announcer from bringing on guests and failed to stop the dancers from horning in with production numbers.

There was a lot of improvising on *The Bette Davis Show*. Alistair Tessier, the announcer, was known to propose as the next guest anyone from Mae West to Captain Ahab, and sometimes one of the queens would rush the set and, impersonating the guest Alistair had introduced, break into art. We in the studio audience were allowed to heckle Bette; it seemed sensible, because, as portrayed by Phil, she had style without content. In fact, except for the interloping dancers, *The Bette Davis Show* was a place with no there in it except for the occasional piquant calamity. A running gag found Bette coming on to declare, very grandly, "Andt now…," to which we would all feign exasperation to cry, "And *when*?" Once, to pacify us, Bette grew sentimental and said, "Some of you may ask why I do this show," and Kenny Fox called out, "Some of us ask *if* you do this show!"

The dancers did more than Bette did. It was somehow understood that the title of each production number answered to a scan of seven syllables accented on the second and sixth, the title itself broken into the name of the dance, followed by its generical description.

Thus, Bette would cry, "Andt now, whadt a treadt for everybutty, as the Bette Davisettes present their interpretation of 'The Punch and Judy Polka.'" The l in *Polka* was not only pronounced but emphasized. "The Bette Davisettes, ladties andt gentlemen!"

And everyone would dash "onstage" to hum vaguely and fling himself around for a bit, then to make a mass exit while singing, "As we dance to 'The Punch and Judy Polka!'"

"Luffly," Bette would cry out, leading—in fact exclusively offering—the applause as the dancers raced back to the couches.

"Encore!" shouts Bert Reed.

"*I'll* be the judge of thadt!" Bette rasps.

Meanwhile, the announcer would try to bring on the usual has-been guest—most often Gale Storm or the Ritz Brothers, although the first time I caught the show it was David Rabe, the playwright known for his Vietnam plays in the 1970s.

"David Rape?" Bette echoed. "Who's he? Some actor!"

No matter, for the dancers again flooded the scene, now to favor us with "The Harvest Moon Cachucha." While they pirouetted off on the line "As we dance to 'The Harvest Moon Cachucha!'" Bette reappeared, looking dangerous.

"The Punch and Judyettes, ladties andt gentlemen!" she almost spat out. "And now—"

"But *when*?" we shouted.

And the dancers tumbled right back onstage for "The Shantytown Gavotta." This time, Bette didn't get out of the way; she held center stage, seething. When the ensemble finally got lost to "As we dance to 'The Shantytown Gavotta,'" Bette cried, "The Shantytown Towelettes, ladties andt gentlemen! And if I never see them again, it will be much too soon! But now…time for sermonette!"

Assuming a spiritual pose, Bette came downstage with "Yes, the devotional part of our show, to comfort heardts in tormendt. This evening's text will be…the first date of Jutter and Lyle!"

And the variety show evaporated, as each queen offered his version of what must have happened, simultaneously editing everyone else's version. The accounts now supported and now contradicted one another, as we learned how unprepared was our boy Jutter for Lyle's notion of true love ways.

"Is 'work you over' just a phrase, or does Lyle really—"

"And Jutter! So *shy*! All those hairy-chested tattoo boys are, you know. Butch in the streets, whimpering in the sheets."

"Lyle has his patented script! He's as rehearsed as Jay Leno, so if you know how to play along…"

"No, Lyle is never satisfied till he glimpses alarm in your eyes!"

"How would *you* know?"

"His mail carrier just *happens to be* my dietician's cousin, and *he* says—"

I jumped in right here with "Lyle is actually a blend of tough and tender, and you never know which you'll get. That's how he lures you into his scene. He seduces you into trusting him to do untrustworthy things to you."

Everyone went silent. Everyone was watching me and stealing quizzical glances at Jason.

"Don't take me wrong," I went on. "Lyle keeps it medically correct. But he is extremely possessive. He demands that you give up everything for him. Then, if you're willing to, he suddenly can't use you. He doesn't love surrender. He loves resistance. That's why he talks about putting on the gloves and going a few rounds—to keep you worried. There's nothing to depend on when you're involved with Lyle, and sooner or later you will yearn to give him up and go with someone safe. But you mustn't. You must never lose Lyle. Because, if you do, for the rest of your life, you'll never know who you really are."

In the long silence that followed, Alistair put a hand over his heart and Bert Reed shook his right fingers in the Italian gesture for awe.

But "Fiddlesticks!" Phil retorted.

"The very *notion*," Alistair agreed, quickly removing his hand.

"What happens," Bert ventured, "when Lyle

meets another Lyle?"

"Were there two Napoleons?" I countered.

"I *scoff*," Phil insisted.

"And who's *your* informant?" Bert asked me.

I shrugged.

Jason was what one might call a queen of respect in this setting, so his friends were somewhat forbearing with me, for all their skepticism. But Jason knows me of old, and when the others are elsewhere he can say anything he wants to me. So he asks: where did I come by this information, anyway? This business of Lyle as…as everyone's gay destiny. It was all so fantastic, so romantic, and so uncomfortably plausible. Yes. It is all that. I sympathized with his confusion. But I wouldn't say any more.

Curiosity was killing him. "Don't we have a bond?" he asked me later that night, when we were alone.

"A bond?" I echoed. I was in a jokey mood that night, and decided to unwind a bit. "Yes, our bond. And it all began with a shared experience when the Wilkes-Barre Little Theatre put on *Light Up the Sky* and your mother played the lead while my father played her husband. She was all over the place for three acts while my dad had just a few lines in one scene when all the other characters were enjoying a nasty rowdydow. Through it all, my dad was sitting on a couch holding a balloon on a stick, his head swinging from left to right and a comically amazed look on his face as he followed the argument. The audience ate it up and gave him the biggest hand of the evening. For which your parents didn't speak to my parents for three years—and this, for some reason, made us pals for life. Our bond."

"Why did you leave Manhattan?" he suddenly asked me. "You haven't really said yet. Not *really*, I mean."

We were driving along the main road through town that eventually becomes the county highway, dropping me off because I hadn't yet bought a car. Another thing about small-town gay life: the gang chores up into workday car pools and special-event chauffeuring without question, as if living in a nineteenth-century commune with ideals and a vision.

"I left Manhattan," I finally told him, "because two men can like and respect each other a very great deal yet never be suited. So we must part, my darling. And yet…life away from the loved one is isolating. So one comes looking for that which one has lost."

"'That which one has lost,'" he repeated, as if trying to scan the concept by chewing on the words.

"Perhaps," I went on, "to find it again in a different form, so to be suited at last."

"I never know what you're talking about," he replied. "Is that me? What you lost?"

I didn't answer. We rode past the diner on my corner, and as he braked I hastily leaned over to peck his cheek. Then I got out and went into my place.

JASON:

I *ask* you! Such *riddles* of life in our *sideshow metropolis*! And meanwhile, there was the Lyle-Jutter thing, and the queens all *agog*, and the *stories* being *told*!

Such as: by the third date with Lyle, Jutter was unnerved. By the fifth...*petrified*! And by the seventh—*hiding out in an undisclosed location*! Well, actually, just an overnight at Todd Rifflin's. During which who knows what went on? Although when you asked Todd, he simply flashed one of his CinemaScope grins and made some festive retort.

And. They. Say. That...Lyle left *six* phone messages on Jutter's answering machine, ranging from annoyed through angry to interplanetary. It seems that our Lyle was not used to being vanished on. No, *Lyle* does the vanishing, doesn't he?

The sermonette segment on *The Bette Davis Show* all but devoured the show itself, because we had so many unsubstantiated rumors to coordinate. And good old Rick—to whom we eagerly turned for those reports that he seemed to pull like rabbits out of his hat—suddenly went mute. He claimed he didn't know any more than we did.

Then, all of a sudden, Jutter was back behind the bar at Mary's as if nothing had happened. So that was nice. And one night, Jutter spent his first break chatting with Rick. And that was...*unbecredible*! How did those two even *know* each other?

Well! The queens were blown *sky-high*! Did this summit meeting of the town's favorite boy and my own personal Rick betoken some new helping of dish soon to be shared? Each of us sort of wandered by them to eavesdrop at various times, but then *of course* they would just happen to be in the middle of analyzing the films of Toffanetti, or whoever that is. You know—the Italian with the clowns? Right. At this crucial turn of events in the history of our lives, that's what Rick and Jutter were fascinated by—the cinema of Toffanetti!

Then Alistair Tessier got a brainstorm. (Allegedly.) It seems that when Mahantango Mary's first opened, the proprietor found his way into some time capsule somewhere and took away a lifetime's supply of those paper placemats from the 1950s with pictures of cocktails next to their recipes. There was always a pile of them on the bar, and they happened to be right where Jutter and Rick were talking. So Alistair said he always wanted to know about a drink called an Angel's Tip, and this looked like his golden opportunity to find out all about this drink. See, he would hang around by the placemats with the apparent intention of showing Jutter how to make an Angel's Tip by pointing to its recipe—because who would know how to make an Angel's Tip otherwise? And, la, while he was waiting to get Jutter's attention, Alistair could…you know. Listen in.

Well, of course, we were all so eager to find out what was going on between Jutter and Rick and that we one and all renounced a golden chance to pass heartless remarks to Alistair on the subject of Angel's Tips. And we shooed him off.

Away he went to spy. *Yes*! But, almost immediately, Jutter's break was over, and he got back behind the bar with the cracked ice and tiny olives, leaving Alistair looking ridiculous with his placemats. At least Rick joined us, so we could pester him with questions. He told us little, because Jutter had secured a vow of confidence. *Of course*!

Worse than that, Rick started lecturing us on not judging the nature of other people's relationships. Not because it's unfair—because it's impossible to know what any two people have. They couldn't tell you themselves, Rick said. They say, He's so hot. Or He makes me laugh, or We see the world in the same way.

"That's cartoon love," Rick told us. "Caption love." (As Phil made low noises, with a sarcastic intention.) Rick said, "What if he's so hot that the way he seizes you in bed centers you so that all else in life is sheer distraction? What if he makes you laugh so easily and happily that you feel liberated in flight with him? The stars *below* you! And what if the two of you see the world in such unity that you feel defended as never yet before? It's marvelous and unearthly—yet it still doesn't tell us much about love, does it? No one knows the truth about love. Most people never even learn the lies."

Yes, he talks like that sometimes. And we were far enough along in the majesty of our goblets not to need to fight with him, and the evening wound down as the drinkers of soda pop and seltzer got ready to play designated driver.

One thing did happen before we all left: Jutter came over to say good night especially to Rick, and to thank him for listening. We queens instantly went on dish alert, and the two of them shook hands—porn stars don't kiss except when working—and Rick said, "Good night, Arthur."

"*Well*!" That boy was scarcely out of hearing before we all had to know. *Arthur*?

"What did you expect?" said Rick. "Did you think a Mr. and Mrs. Flexx had a son they named Jutter?"

What's the rest of it?" asked Phil.

"Driscoll. Arthur Driscoll."

RICK:

And Jutter insisted that I call him that. Arthur. It's hard to separate him from his model name, though, because he had such impact as Jutter Flexx. Yes, he was a fine fellow and all that: but he was also photography. To treat him as mortal dwindled his myth. And how many of us can even claim one in the first place?

Some porn models love embodying a fantasy. It's not just work for money; it's ennoblement. But if Jutter had once been keen to command a following, by the time he came to live *among* us he had truly come to live among us: as just a guy you know, with pals and pastimes. He says the reason he fought off all offers to cast him in what he called "action" videos is that he didn't enjoy being a dreamboy after all.

"I'm only a sex model on the outside," he once told me. "Inside, I'm just as confused and broke as everybody else. What about that junkheap on wheels that I ride around in—when it runs? Is that part of the…the magic of…Yes, or that dump I live in, so small it's hidden by two fir trees? Whose place is that? Rumpelstilskin's? If I'm so lucky, how come I can't get a decent night's sleep?"

And I was like, Huh?

He nodded. "Insomnia. For years now. It takes forever for me to zonk out, and two hours later I'm stone-cold awake all over again. Then I'm dragging myself around all the next day."

There was a pause, and then he said, "Arthur Driscoll," as if that explained something. "Everyone thinks porn is empowering to you. They think…Yeah, but what ignorance, you know? Did porn empower Brad Wagner? He killed himself in prison because he was facing DNA proof on multiple counts of hetero rape."

I just looked at him, waiting for clarification. Brad Wagner?

"You would know him as Tim Barnett," he said.

"I don't think I would know him at all, actually."

"He was a nice guy, too. I used to meet him at parties, when he'd come out west to shoot a film." Seeing my continued lack of comprehension, he underlined it: "Tim Barnett, the porn star? Classic Falcon type? Handsome and really built, with that light brown hair only Falcon models have. Everybody liked him. A sworn bottom, very into the sex of it all. Even a good actor, though he told me that in all his films he'd had but the one dialogue scene. He played a psychiatrist in love with his patient. That big blond boy Ty Fox. Did Tim Barnett have it all? That's what they say about porn stars, don't they? They're the sweethearts of the world. Yeah…a sweetheart and a rapist. Have it all? He never got to forty!"

We were sitting in his car, outside my house. Jutter had given me a lift home, because he needed someone to talk to. I'm a good listener. Not everyone is, you know. To listen to a guy…really listen, now…you have to empty your head of all its content, all the intel about *you*, and let someone else pour his stuff inside. Some folks cannot bear leaving their private alternate universe even for a minute.

"You have a nice place," he said suddenly, way off-topic. "I'll bet you don't have any trouble sleeping through the night."

After a pause, I ventured to observe that Lyle is a bit like a porn star in that he has a public and a legend.

"Yes, Lyle." He sighed. "Magical man. And so…worrying. And yet when I'm next to him in bed I get a full night's sleep." He chipped out a laugh. "Like that for irony? No insomnia with Lyle. I lie in bed with a man like him and I go right into dreamyland and don't come back till he wakes me the next morning. He roughs up my hair and says, 'Come along, sleepyhead.' Isn't that a posting on your Facebook wall? And when he gets all ruthless on me and threatens me, he grabs my dick and of course it's hard. I can't help it, he's so fucking *man*. And he'll squeeze my hand around his dick, and he's hard, too. 'See that?' he says. 'We're two of a kind and you *want* me running you.'"

After a moment, he asked me, "What's it like to be just his friend, I wonder?"

And I answered, "It's a lot easier than being his boy friend."

JASON:

Well, let's all say thank you to our ever so wonderfully enigmatic Rick and his share in the narrative, filled with more mysteries than when Scheherazade threw Alfred Hitchcock his Sweet Sixteen party. But now it's time to get to The Night Lyle and Jutter Had It Out, for the queens have been singing this song to and fro in town ever since.

To be blunt: some five or six weeks after Jutter and Lyle broke up—or, as some of us more precisely put it, after Jutter ran *screaming in terror* from Lyle's menacing embrace—we were all in the bar, waiting for something to happen. Alistair Tessier was so enchanted by the drinks deconstructed on those idiotic placemats that he was sampling them, one a night. On the evening of which I speak, he was working on a Napoleon Tarantella (which sounds like a dance number from *The Bette Davis Show*). Jutter was quietly tending his half of the bar. A slow night for all.

Till Lyle Hickock walked in.

Well!

Call us queens if you will—and you *must*!—but, all the same, we are professionals, ready to execute our three sacred missions:

Watch.

Report.

Exaggerate.

Suddenly: "Freeze," whispered Alistair, breathless as a spy. "Don't any of us move till Lyle reaches the placemats." Todd Rifflin was the first to take action. He went up to Lyle and started stretching his limbs to show off—in a see-through mesh top and fatigues, no less! You know the shtick—"I upped my weight setting at the gym and I think I might have pulled something."

What a ham! Yet Lyle appeared to be buying it, reaching out an appreciative—yet strangely dispassionate—hand to inspect Todd's abs while Todd treated Lyle to his patented "You like me, right?" smile. Oh, that *giddy* bundle of blond *confusions*! You know how Todd describes his orientation? "Bi-flexible," he calls it. I *mean*, did you *ever*?

And poor Jutter had to witness all this, sure that Lyle was just using Todd. Because every soul in the bar knew that our Lyle hadn't come to Mary's to admire that tempty-teasy showgirl Todd Rifflin. No, my friends. Lyle had come to *claim his boy*! And don't think that Jutter didn't know it, watching Lyle and Todd hitting it off and feeling like Ethel Merman bound and gagged as her understudy sneaks on in *Flower Drum Schlong*.

And then, as we played witness in the sheer joy of learning the history as it is made before our very eyes, Jutter snapped at last. You could almost hear the very sound of it as he vaulted *right! over! the bar*! I mean, he leaped into the air past the little umbrellas and fruit slices and plastic swizzle sticks and landed with a thump on the floor just behind Lyle, as if to turn—no, *whirl* him around and cry, "Okay, just what is it that you may be up to hereabouts, my fine fellow?" Or whatever those he-men say when they're all jammed up about love and jealousy.

Jutter's Leap is how we refer to it now, in our fond nostalgia, and it led Phil Conroy to envision a gay Olympics, no less. But no, I mean a real gay Olympics, with gay events. Like, instead of the shot put, you'd compete in how far you could throw your cheating boy friend's rare cast-album CDs out the apartment window. Or you'd go for the gold in Jutter's Leap.

Meanwhile. Lyle now turned to look at Jutter for the first time that evening, and of course Lyle's expression was inscrutable. How do you think these smoldering demigods get legendary in the first place? The rest of us were completely spectating, naturally. Would Jutter make some sort of submissive gesture? Would Lyle caveman him out of the place? We were *breathless* and *rooted to the spot*.

And just then, good old Rick decided to butt in and change everything around.

RICK:

I didn't change anything. But Lyle and Arthur needed a referee. Lyle would be sore, because despite his phlegmatic self-presentation he really does have a temper. The moment called for finesse.

Really, I just wanted to help.

JASON:

You help? Who are you, the World Health Organization? Besides, when do we learn what your strangely unidentified role in all this is?

RICK:

We will, my sweet, but for the moment I have the continuity: and it turns out that Lyle and Arthur did not need any help, except in my spiriting off the clinging Todd. In fact, with Todd out of the way the two of them apparently got into one of those more or less neutral chats, a bit of catchup in the lightest of tones. True, I had an inkling that they weren't going to stay neutral once they were out of public view. But at least D-Day was not in the current rotation schedule. So I dragged Todd away, on his favorite pretext…

JASON:

Sex for money? Because within minutes you two were nowhere to be found.

RICK:

…and left Lyle and Arthur talking it over. And, I am told, the bar manager let Arthur quit early, so Lyle offered him a ride home. And off the two of them went.

But that, truly, is when The Night began. Because Lyle had no intention of dropping Arthur off. When he drove past Franklin Street, Arthur said, "You missed the turn."

Lyle did not respond to that. One block later, he had to stop for a red light, and Arthur saw that Lyle's eyes were raging like a sci-fi super-villain's, as brilliant as a surprise in the plot. Arthur tried to slip out of his seat belt to lam out of the truck, but Lyle reached over and grabbed him, saying, "You sit tight or I'll slam my fist into your face so hard you won't come back for a month."

And that's how they rode the rest of the way to Lyle's: the big guy smoking like Vesuvius and Arthur apprehensive but considering his options.

JASON:

As they danced to "The Lyle Hickock Fandango!"

Well! There are so many different, dare I say *editions* of the tale that *we* refer to it as the Gospel. Because Phil Conroy *insisted* that when Lyle and Jutter pulled into the driveway of Lyle's spread—because Lyle's house sits right next to Hickock Motors, I suppose the better to imprison you, my dear—the host said he was going to take Jutter inside, fix his wagon good in the traditional Lyle manner, and then kick him out. Yes, in the middle of the night! We have a policy, sir! And to make sure that Jutter didn't try to zip off again, Lyle pulled him out of the car on the driver side and threatened to wreck him on the spot if he called for help. Phil said a neighbor saw the whole thing from her kitchen window.

But Alistair Tessier claimed that Jutter broke away after all, and Lyle had to chase him and tackle him and drag him inside kicking, with Lyle's hand over Jutter's mouth. According to Alistair, his cable guy or something just happened to be passing and witnessed the event. While drinking an Angel's Tip, no doubt.

But Bert Reed said that once Lyle got Jutter inside and into Lyle's room, he stripped them both while Jutter begged and pleaded. *Ha*! The sound of music to a sadist's ears! And then! Taking out an English boarding-school birch rod, Lyle laid it ceremonially on the bed, turned to Jutter, and said,

"C'm'ere."

Okay, so far so good—but how do we *know*? We were at Phil's, this was, arguing over whose book of Gospel was *the* book, or at least the most likely, or at any rate the most fun, when everyone sort of turned to my good old comrade Rick. And *he* said

RICK:

They settled it in the car, actually. There's a small parking lot between the house and the business, and, after Lyle pulled in there and turned the car off, he started a new conversation. He was still angry, but at least now he left out the threatening overtones.

First, Lyle asked Arthur why he broke it off without confronting him. And Arthur replied, sensibly, that Lyle was too rough with him, and extremely volatile when things don't go his way. So a confrontation wouldn't have been a good idea. Worse, Arthur feared that, in Lyle's presence, all his resistance would have evaporated. Because he knew deep in his tender little human heart that he would never be happy unless he could sleep peacefully next to Lyle. And Arthur told Lyle that, straight out, and Lyle replied that, in that case, Arthur might just as well give up this foolishness and move in with Lyle.

"I don't like that stupid little house you're in, anyway," said Lyle. "It's cold and wet and it's in the wrong part of town. It's hours wasted every week, going back and forth. Tomorrow we'll take the pickup over and pile your stuff in and bring you back here. You'll quit that bar job and make yourself useful around the shop, learn a trade like a man."

Resistance is futile, as they put it on television. You will be assimilated.

Never softening even in victory, Lyle went on, "I can teach you a few things about auto tech, turn a glamour boy into a real guy about town. You'll be grateful eventually. And Jeff and Desi will adopt you as one of their own."

"Desi?" Arthur asked.

"Don't get cute about my business associates," said Lyle. Altogether, this scene in his car found him saying more than he usually does in a whole week.

Well, so I shared this with Jason and his chums. I told them that Lyle habitually chose his partners by a code known only to himself, but that this time Lyle himself was chosen. Love chose him. Arthur chose him, not because Lyle was raw and wild but because, when Arthur got close to him, he felt so secure that he could lie in those arms and rest.

And, once again, the queens were silent. They liked their Gospel, but they liked mine better. Finally Jason got it:

JASON:

"You didn't come here to look me up," I told Rick, driving him home that night. "You came to find Lyle. You're one of his exes, and that explains all this…subterfuge. Am I right?"

"Yes, actually."

"So all your information," I further concluded, "comes straight from Lyle?"

"Some from Arthur."

"So."

We drove a bit without speaking, till I asked him, "Did he beat you up? Lyle? *Really* beat you?"

"Not really. He has his overwhelming side, I suppose. In the end, though, he's less a bully than a stone idol. On the other hand, he does play rough."

"Why?"

"Men that sexy are crazy," he replied. "Sex is crazy. Gays are crazy. It's our gift."

So now we know. Anyway, Jutter and Lyle have been together ever since, about two years now. They don't get out much, so even Rick doesn't see them to any extent. Jutter has been learning about fixing cars and Lyle runs Hickock Motors more or less all day plus, so what those two do in their spare time is anybody's guess. Maybe they play cop show, with Jeff and Desi as this week's guest suspects, and it's all very sneaky and realistic. Rick says that, as he understands it, they're devoted to each other and live in a state of unquestioning mutual respect. Allegedly. But the main thing is that theatrical improvisations based on their saga have become even more popular at Phil Conroy's At Homes than *The Bette Davis Show*.

Sometimes I get to play Jutter. My favorite moment comes when Phil, playing Lyle, announces that I must now learn about carburetors and dipsticks and oiling mechanics in the hood, and I always reply, "How many of them do I oil?," which breaks everybody up. So, you see, life is back to normal in our little gay town.

And one evening, when I was driving Rick home—yes, he *still*¬ doesn't drive his own car—I asked him, out of the blue, if I he thought I would ever meet someone like Lyle and be able to slumber in his arms in perfect union—as Lyle and…all right, *Arthur*…are probably doing as we speak. Rick knew I wasn't fishing for consolations. I wanted the truth, and only a friend-for-life can give you that.

And he answered, "No."

I nodded. Yes, well. No Lyle for this boy. Rick kissed my cheek as he got out, and I drove on home. And when I opened the door, both cats came running up to say how much they'd missed me, which they had never done before.

THE FLIPPETY FLOP

The big black sailor was sitting alone, way down at the far end of the bar. It was after midnight on a Thursday. The place was quiet, as turned off as an Edward Hopper. Richard took the stool next to the sailor as casually as possible, ordered a Johnny Walker Red on the rocks, and waited.

"Man," said the sailor at last, in a softly rolling undertone. "This sure is a mean city of a place."

Richard nodded, his head but half turned to the man, his eyes lowered. He didn't like staring directly into a stranger's eyes, or other such…assertive behavior.

"Set up this shore leave to stay with an ol' girl friend, suddenly she get all teasy an' agitated, throw my ass right out of there. Now I'm stuck for bunkin' room."

Trying his can of Bud, the sailor found it empty and banged it on the edge of the bar with a murmured,

"Fuck that shit." Clasping his hands before him, turning them palms out to stretch the joins of his upper body in his summer whites, he added, "Seem like everythin' goin' wrong this night."

"Can I buy you another?" Richard asked, turning to face the man but still avoiding a direct gaze. The sailor looked right at him as if trying to draw his eyes, center the meeting. Richard dared a quick look then, scarcely even a glance, really, but enough to see the sailor's unsettling half-smile. Idly looking back down at his drink, Richard heard him say, "Now, that would make a nice start."

Richard signaled the bartender.

"Well, yeah," the sailor went on, swivelling on his stool to allow Richard, in a series of darting inspections, to take him in. Bending his arms and thrusting them back to emphasize his massive chest development, broadening his smile. When the beer arrived, he tipped the can at Richard by way of thanks, took a swig, wiped his mouth with his free hand, and asked, "What do you want to know?"

"I can see that you're one of those bodybuilders," said Richard, now forcing himself to focus on the sailor's face. "I shouldn't think life on a ship would give you a lot of gym time. Or…even…do they *have* gyms on boats?"

"They got everythin' on boats, son," said the sailor, parking his beer can as if embarking on a serious lecture. "Tell you truth, they ain' much to do at sea when you're off duty, 'cep watch TV or play cards. Or lift. Hell, I be in that gym every day. Two, three hours' worth."

"Yes, you…really look it."

"Feel this," the sailor half-whispered, tightening his left biceps about an inch in front of Richard's face. "See how big like you could taste it. Go ahead."

Hastily looking around to see if anyone was spying on them, Richard obliged. He took a good long squeeze of the sailor's arm, saying, "That's quite something."

"Lot more on me where that come from, too," the sailor added, conspiratorially. "I'm gen'rally big. Guarantee."

The two of them went on for a while on a number of topics, Richard playing it neutral and the sailor constantly edging in with an angle. His girl friend throwing him out. The cost of a room. Finally, he said, "You seem like a nice guy, you know? Feel I can trus' you. Seein' as I got no place tonight, how's about I bunk in with you?"

"That would be fine," said Richard. "In fact, I live rather nearby. Just—"

"Le's shove off."

They left the bar and started walking, the sailor setting the pace at a confident amble. Neither said anything till they were inside Richard's apartment.

"Nice joint," said the sailor, though he wasn't looking around. He was looking at Richard. "What you got for us to drink?"

"I'm out of beer, I'm afraid. There's…well, let's see…"

"I'll have what you're havin'."

"Is scotch okay?"

"Take mine neat," said the sailor, parking himself on the couch.

When Richard brought the glasses out of the

kitchen, the sailor said, “Yeah, this ol’ girl friend, like I say—thank you, my man—she get real problematical. Time and again, you know?”

“Yes,” Richard replied, joining the man on the couch.

“She, like, whackin’ on my program. Can’t get a step right, they in that mood. You know?”

“Yes.”

“Shucks, I *know* she fussin’ ‘cause I want to do the flippety flop and she don’t care to take it up the ass. Sure. Lick her candy, suck up her boobs, pussy-fuck her. Then she all ‘Oh, honey boy, tha’s so fly. Tha’s so true.’ Yeah, she do surely *love* that usual shit. But when I ask her to flop for me please, she give me shade straight up. She like ‘You outta here *pronto*!’”

“I…the flippety flop?”

The sailor smiled broadly and put his arm around Richard’s shoulders, buddy-style. “Well, sure, tha’s what this man’s navy call sex. Rear motion. She on her back, legs high, as you move to the rhythm of love.” Murmuring into Richard’s ear, the sailor said, “Le’s whisper now. Like the ol’ song go:

> You be the bottom,
> I be the top,
> When we do the flippety flop.

Taking a sip of his drink, the sailor added, “Know what I mean?”

Richard’s face was so close to the sailor’s that he felt a bit dizzy, and he decided to steady himself by putting a hand, very gently, flat against the sailor’s chest.

"Yep," the sailor continued. "One go flip and the other go flop. Tha's the song of the world, I venture to say. Song of the world, hear? And yet I be so put out when my lady go and front me like so, 'specially when I got a heavy case of the flips for her. An', son, I'm tellin' you, that sweet miss flop real tight and tasty when she be willin' to."

Winking at Richard, the sailor threw back a big swallow, his arm so heavy on Richard that the two of them seemed to move together like a dance team. Easing his way onto his feet, the sailor announced, "Here I go to fix me a shower. Okay for you?"

"Be my guest, please."

The sailor was already pulling off his clothes. "Yeah, 'cause now I'm overheated through…jus' a minute here with the tunic…through sufferin' the flips for my lady Miss Tina. Too biggety for me, I guess. Or I don't know. Get a guy full of rush and then…these buttons here…don' know why they don't jus'…then deck me flat, you know?"

Richard, staring as the man's body gradually hove into view, said nothing.

"Man," said the sailor, not to Richard as much as in general, as a public-service announcement, "I got the flips so fierce tonight that someone bes' flop for me soon, or there surely be trouble at the crossroads."

Then he breezed into the bathroom. Richard remained on the couch, slipping off his loafers and drinking his scotch as the narrative cues told from the bathroom: a quick whiz, humming, the water smacking down from the shower nozzle. Always the same theme in Richard's life: dark-alley giants, suspicious and spiky—or, even worse, friendly, but with a catch. How did you get there, Richard? The cheap music is supposed to be potent, not fearsome.

"Got this sorta crunch in my neck," said the sailor when he came back, lazily toweling off like a model. "S'pose you could step up behin' an' take care of that for me?"

Richard put down his drink and rose as the sailor turned away for a neck rub, tossing the towel aside and then breathing out delighted gasps as Richard worked on him. More humming.

"See how I got all dry for you?" the sailor said. "Way up more the right side, now."

Richard followed instructions, massaging the sailor's thick neck and shoulders.

"An' try my sides, too," he urged. "Go far with it."

He let his head loll forward, his eyes closed, enjoying the attention in a kind of reverie. Then Richard slowly ran his hand across the man's stomach, and he snapped to, turning to grab Richard in rough play and push him back onto the couch, following the movement along so that he had Richard in a virtual embrace. Smiling, he reached for Richard's drink and held it before them as if teasing Richard in some arcane ritual. He took a sip, put the glass down, gently tapped on the end of Richard's nose, and said, "Where was we before? Do you recall, now?"

Richard was silent, his hands resting on the sailor's sides.

"Oh, yeah. We was considerin' the fine points of the flippety flop. Remember? Now me, I prefer a partner who got to be a little talked into it, like they 'fraid of it even though they want it. That give me a chance to sing to 'em, like I showed you before. You like my singin'?"

Richard nodded.

"An' what's your name, f'I ain' too personal?"

"Richard."

"Hello, there, Richard," said the sailor, stroking Richard's hair. "I'm Norman."

"It's nice to meet you, Norman. You're a…an extraordinary-looking man."

The sailor's eyes went sharp as slate as he forced Richard's head back, and he moved closer as if to kiss Richard but veered off suddenly to whisper into Richard's ear, "Listen at this new verse of the flippety flop song."

Now he took hold of Richard with both hands, pressing him close while keeping his mouth on Richard's ear.

"You listenin', now?"

"Yes," said Richard.

"Okay, now, Richard, here it go:

You be the bottom,
Pump you till you pop,
When we do the flippety flop.

Do you love my tuneful song?" the sailor went on, reaching down to unbutton Richard's shirt. "Way I figger it, that melody tell about showin' your secret soft side. See, it ain' only ladies who get the flops. Guys do, too, though they don' like to admit it. They give escuses, fearful ol' Norman there'll goin' to enjoy hisself too much."

Reaching the bottom button of Richard's shirt,

the sailor grabbed it out of his pants, freed the sleeves, and peeled the shirt off him.

"Do…" Richard began, but his voice faltered. Starting again: "Do any of the men on your ship get the flops?"

"Time after time," replied the sailor, lazily running his hands over Richard's torso. "'Specially one fine blond boy named Chipper. I call him Chipewee when we alone. I knew he had the flops for me, but he too scared to open up."

"But surely…I mean…a crowded Navy ship doesn't give you privacy…does it?"

"Shucks, they's plenty of secret places. And I got *engenyuity*. Once, I catch Chip when no one's aroun,' fasten up the place, and sing to the boy. Pretty soon, he jus' weepin' how he got the flops and *please* don' flip him."

"Did you?"

Stroking Richard's hair, the sailor didn't answer. He was hard now, and when he caught Richard staring, he smiled and licked his lips.

"But did you flip him, Norman?"

Resting a hand on Richard's neck, the sailor broke into a wide smile. "Sure I did. That the best flip of all, when they grow fearful 'bout the ways of love."

Tugging Richard's trousers open, the sailor held him against the couch with his left hand on Richard's breastbone while stripping him from the waist down.

"There. Now we both clean simple, we can talk honest to each other."

"Please don't hurt me."

"Won't hurt you none, be you honest. 'Cause I suspect you got the flops for me, an' I want you to confess up."

"I don't have the...the flops, Norman. I'm almost positive I don't."

"You don' want to front me, now," said the sailor with a disquietingly tender air. "'Cause I get pretty heavy on those who deny they true wish. I seen you eyin' me up before."

"I swear, Norman."

"Well, you beat all, son." Shaking his head incredulously: can you *believe* it? "Callin' me by my name yet lyin' right to my eyes about havin' the flops. Now I espect I best check you out in the time-honor way, an' if I find you lyin' I don' know what I'll do."

The sailor pulled Richard to his feet and hustled him into the bedroom, resting one hand on Richard's head as he yanked back the bedclothes.

"Please, Norman, I don't have the flops. I'm really quite sure about that now."

"Then you got nothin' to worry 'bout," said the sailor, taking hold of Richard by the sides and forcing him, rather casually, onto his back on the bed. "I don' flip a guy less he got the flops." Looking around, he fastened upon the little drawer in the night table next to the bed. "Ho, what do we see? Got your works in here?" An overacted smile superintended the opening of the drawer in a slow tease, followed by the discovery of—as the sailor put it—"joygrease and the condom box."

Taking them out and then straddling the silent, unmoving Richard, the sailor beamed down at him with "Le's taste your kisses, find out do you got the flops after all. I can tell by the flavor."

Now Richard entered into it, reaching up for the

sailor as he swooped down to feast upon Richard's lips. A connoisseur. "Yeah," the sailor murmured, as Richard responded with helpless passion. "You're a tiger now, givin' it up to me." He sounded pleased, but when his head came up a bit later his look was angrily aggrieved. Richard loved that part.

"You been holdin' out on me, Jack, tell that from the taste o' you. Gone to have to wreck you just a bit." Backing off Richard's body, he said, "Get those legs high, 'cause you got the flops and it be full steam ahead. Huh." Then: "Jus' a *little* grease," he explained, "so you can feel this to the heart o' you." As he cracked open a condom, he paused to note, "The night was made for love, son. But this be the tough kin'."

Nevertheless, the sailor handled Richard gently, almost protectively. He kept up a patter of lewd encouragement, praising Richard's "suction technique" and raving over his "liplock" as they closed up tight for the "kiss an' come." Richard himself remained silent to the end, when his lord breathed out, "Here go the flyin' part" and crashed through moon and stars—Richard glimpsed them in the man's lidded eyes as he threw his head back—to spend and droop and fall over, panting.

They lay there for some minutes then, utterly blank to each other, bodies without character. Then the sailor raised his head, patted Richard's stomach, jumped up, retrieved his clothing from the living room, returned, dropped the clothes on a chair, and went into the bathroom for a second shower. Going over the evening's events like a man reprieved for thoughtcrime, Richard stayed put. He had not come, but he'd take care of that part later in nostalgic privacy. As always.

Norman came out of the bathroom, toweling off as before. “So,” he said. “How do you think the vocab worked? I’ve been practicing on my friends—they probably think I’m rehearsing for something by August Wilson.”

“The contractions kind of came and went, I thought,” said Richard, still floating back to earth. “But Chipewee was wonderfully sinister. I think you slipped a bit with ‘The night was made for love,’ though.”

“How so?” asked Norman, starting to get back into uniform.

“It’s a Jerome Kern song.”

“Yeah, the…shoot, why’re there so many buttons on…the *Show Boat* guy?”

“It skewed the tone a bit. Oh, but the part about tasting my kisses to see if I had the flops was sensational.”

“Lock that in?”

“Roger.”

Half-dressed, Norman breezed over to the desk, where Richard had left four hundred dollars in twenties, fanned out and separated into groups of five so Norman didn’t have to count them.

“Same time next month?” Norman asked, pocketing the cash and turning back to Richard with a nice smile, his own this time.

“Well, I’ve got this idea,” said Richard, lazily stirring up the sheets with his feet as he lay in bed. “Mr. Prendergast. Suit and horn rims. Works as the Incentive Man for The Corporation. You know the type. Cool on the outside, but inside…”

"Your friendly neighborhood raging volcano?"

Richard nodded happily. "When a department's earnings go down," he explained, "Mr. Prendergast shows up to discipline the department head."

"You?" Norman asked, turning the uniform tunic around to find the top.

Richard nodded again. "Or there have been too many changes in personnel. It hampers productivity, you see. No, how would they put it? It...threatens market share? Be sure to use the idioms of the parish. They're always talking about money, but they're thinking about sex. You know. *Earnings. Breakout.* It's all pumping and coming. Mr. Prendergast should be the embodiment of that. I see it as an exposé of business life. *Mad Men* with skin."

"Yeah, but...horn rims? Eek." Getting his arms inside the tunic and pulling it over his head, Norman added, " I won't be able to see anything. I'll be having sex with your pants."

"The glasses are central, though. Like the cucumber sandwiches in *The Importance of Being Earnest.*"

"You're the boss."

"You should carry an attaché, too."

Sitting to get on his shoes and socks, Norman asked, "Do you have a CD for me?"

"Oh, surely."

Reaching for a bathrobe draped over the top left bedpost, Richard pulled it on as he rose, then crossed the room to the bookcase. Retrieving a disc in its jewel case, Richard turned, quietly watching Norman finish dressing.

"What?" Norman asked him, grinning.

Instead of replying, Richard simply handed him the CD. Taking it, Norman studied its cover, a rendering of snow-topped Everests in the foreground with, in the distance, a sun feebly radiant in a vast cavern.

"What's this?" Norman asked happily. "The beginning of all things?"

"Or the end. Strauss' *Also Sprach Zarathustra*. A tone poem on the ravings of a sage." With a wry smile, Richard added, "It starts with the 'Theme From *2001: A Space Odyssey*.' You know. Music on the eternal beauty of power."

"Who's this conductor? Is he famous?"

"Giuseppe Sinopoli. Big noise, lots of excitement. No longer with us, unfortunately."

"Nifty. Thanks, Richard."

"Any news, professionally speaking?"

Fastening a shoelace, Norman chuckled. "You won't believe this—an all-black *Salome*."

"The Wilde? Another executioner gig?"

"The Baptist."

"Get *out*!"

"Apparently they have a Krunch outlet in the desert." He stood up, smoothing out the lie of the sleeves of his tunic. "But the director is gay and a half, so anything's possible. They've already signed the Salome. A genuine babe. And they're talking of nudity. So far, I've got an edge."

"Do me a favor? Memorize your part in the Wilde. For the audition, right? Don't let the competition out-prepare you."

"Okay, my friend. Thanks"

"No, thank you. Call me before next month,

because I'll have to arrange the hotel reservation. The scene will be my room during one The Corporation's business conferences. They come from miles around and so on. Mr. Prendergast pays his visits to the errant executives. He likes his work. Very proper, unflappable, a little mysterious. Think of something new, okay? Really frighten me."

"You got it, buddy."

They were standing there.

"Well…"

"Yeah."

"…anyway…"

"Sure."

At the door, they embraced, a nice long one. Richard accidentally let out a sigh, and Norman said, "Richard, you take your fun so *seriously*!"

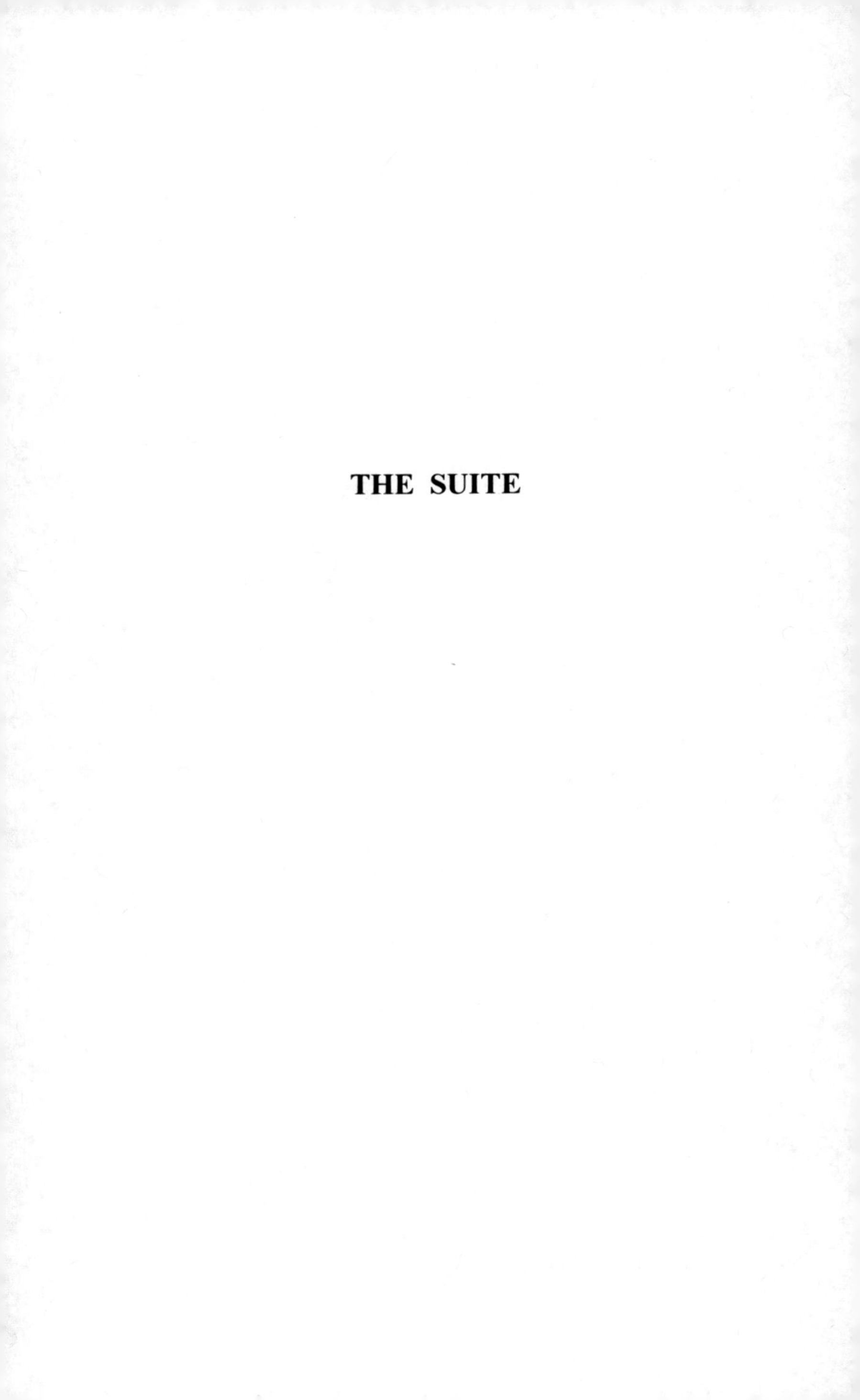

THE SUITE

The usual professional cynics declared that the firm was lavish with quality-of-life extras so the boss could keep an eye on everyone—because no one ever wanted to leave the grounds. The cafeteria, open only to employees and their guests, served the best food in the county. The living quarters, in six huge towers and divvied up by an intricate series of promotions, were loaded with space-age accessories, from the instant ironing valet to the on-demand video-and-music library servicing the entertainment center. The daycare "corrals" were playrooms shelled entirely in glass so parents could effect a moment or two of visual nurturing at any time of day.

That did leave every employee exposed in some way or other to virtual surveillance. Take the twenty-four hour concierge service—was this a blessing of aides or a network of spies? What were they writing in those logs as you walked from the front door to the elevator? And what did the daycare handlers learn about your homelife from your children? Cynics said the apartments were bugged, even screened.

Yet one had to admit that the firm was a great employer. A happy place, even a workers' paradise. It was set out on a sprawling so-called "campus" way past the suburbs in a life so complete in itself that, despite the free-parking garages, most of the staff sold their cars after the first year. Like everything else in the firm, the pay scale was top of the line. Well, *duh*: wasn't this the proudest corporation in the state? It was the fourth biggest in primary billing, and from the way its profits surged in good times and held fast even in bad, quarter to quarter, it would soon rule unrivaled.

Nationally, too, the firm maintained a high-status reputation. In the business world, it was a truth universally acknowledged that nothing smiled upon one's self-esteem like a surprise visit from one of the firm's headhunters. Of course, the firm had its own terms for it: a "talkabout" from a "messenger." It was one of the boss' many innovations. Far more than your mere man of action, he was a scrambler, an improviser. Legend told that his favorite saying was "I want it on my desk last Thursday."

So you would say yes to the messenger, and you and your family (if applicable) got whisked off to headquarters. A very few days later, your personal property would arrive, to be stored in your new furnishings (options: "classic," "cutting edge," "time travel") in your new place in one of the residence towers. Single newcomers, on any but the executive level, were set into two-bedroom flats with a roommate. The cynics: right. Another spy.

C. J. came to the firm with a marketing

background built up more on the job than through an impressive diploma. It was said that the boss, a self-made man, liked others of his kind. Signs were posted all over the office floors of the sort one glimpses in old black-and-white movies: START SOMETHING. Or COMMERCE IS CATCHING. One read, YOU CAN LEARN FROM YOUR WORST ENEMY.

C. J. was twenty-six, and he had been in love three times. All ended badly. His first was in high school: his best friend, Kurt O'Connor. The two boys spent time together in a tree house on an abandoned property, and one afternoon—so suddenly that he scared himself—C. J. kissed Kurt on the cheek. Kurt didn't say anything, but he went home right after and always had something else to do whenever C. J. called.

C. J.'s second love was a professor in C. J.'s first year of community college, a spirited lecturer in English with an unpredictable taste in neckties. The class met at twelve noon each Monday, Wednesday, and Friday, and the professor made a point of lunching directly after with any willing students in the school café. C. J. never missed a lunch, and finally the professor invited C. J. to his apartment to hear his antique jazz LPs. Thus encouraged, C. J. wrote the teacher a letter confessing affection, and the next day he was summoned by his adviser and requested to drop the English course "for personal reasons."

C. J.'s third love was consummated. He met this fellow in a bar two towns down the highway and convinced himself that, because the sex worked, everything else would as well. However, C. J.'s new boy friend was one of those "out" guys, like the ones you see giving pep talks on YouTube, recommending aggressive lifestyle choices. This boy liked to hold hands in the street and whistle at cute men. He also wanted to move in with C. J., and when C. J. told him that would necessitate considerable thought, the boy turned up in C. J.'s town, telling their secrets to strangers. And suddenly the entire universe took one giant step back from C. J. Nobody was rude, exactly. Rather, folks used to be friendly and now they were businesslike. The waitress at C. J.'s luncheonette of choice habitually traded vacuous quips with him, but now she said nothing, and when she left the check she wouldn't meet his eyes.

So, when C. J. got the firm's offer, he jumped at it and lit out of there. It would be all new at the firm, he told himself—a restart of his life, as if he were an e-screen with fresh apps to install. And there was this: the boss' theory of blending work and leisure was so all-encompassing that the firm was in effect one of the biggest cities in the state. Everyone knew that. And that meant C. J. wouldn't be isolated any more, the only one like him or, worse, stuck with crazy versions of himself, like his ex-boy friend the professional gay.

And, right from his first day on campus, the firm welcomed C. J. in exactly this way: he made a connection with someone like himself within seconds of his arrival. It happens that, in another of the boss' innovations, individuals of the executive caste were required to serve as docents, to help the new hires acclimatize themselves. Another of the signs on the office walls read INSPIRATION IS CONTAGIOUS.

It was a Saturday in June, late morning. C. J.'s guide was a fortysomething named Robin, and by the time she was showing him the pools—three of them, one for kiddies, one vast, one vaster—C. J. felt he could Signal.

"Good cruising, I see," he noted, as a gaggle of the bold and beautiful passed in swimsuits, the women bearing pool bags.

Grunting sardonically—and only a lesbian can pull that off—Robin said, "So you guessed, huh? What tipped you off?"

"That little gray streak in your hair," C. J. replied. "It's so…uncompromising?"

"Ha. You're fast, mister. And if you can answer the following question, I'll give you three tips on how to get along around here."

C. J. moved out of the way of a family group: a youngish couple arm in arm, two kids happily trudging along behind them, the entire unit in subdued but unmistakably contented spirits.

"What is this?" C. J. murmured to Robin, "Stepford, U.S.A.?"

"Well, they do treat you up. Did I mention that the ice cream is free?"

"No possible way!"

Robin nodded as, in front of them, in the vaster pool, a showboater in electric-blue trunks effected a glittery swan dive off the high board.

"One pint," Robin went on, "once a month, at the super. You use your emp card, with a wave of the hand over the reader. Any flavor. So. Ready for your question?"

"Hit me."

"No gal has ever revealed this innermost secret of the club, so ponder well, poor deprived male that ye be…Who is the woman that all gals have loved and desired for the last several decades? The *only* one."

Now both C. J. and Robin had to move aside as a bunch of jocks ran past to clump into a mass cannonball and fire into the water, drenching everyone lounging at the water's edge.

"Dibs on the guy in the red trunks," said C. J.

"It's the dire secret," said Robin, focused on her question, "that no dyke has ever revealed to men."

Turning from the water to face Robin, C. J. said, "Give me a hint."

Robin thought for a bit, then uttered one word: "Dummies."

"*Oh*! Candice Bergen!"

"You're good, man. Now the prize. Tip number one: always call your employer 'the boss,' even when you mean your section head or your supervisor. Is there really a boss of this whole shooting match somewhere around here? Isn't there?" Robin shook her head. "We'll never know. Just say it. 'The boss.' It shows you're going with the program."

The two were now walking out of the pool area, heading up to the miniature golf field and the so-entitled Mad Cantina, a snack bar with a rotating menu of ethnic specialties. One day it was Thai and the next Italian; the crusted spaghetti with baby peas outselling even the miniature pizza pies. Midway along the path, a pretty blonde was offering free lollipops out of a wicker basket strapped to her side.

"Sugar-free," Robin noted, to C. J. "Just fruit juice and glue."

"Yes, but…the whole user-friendly atmosphere starts to get…I mean, doesn't it?"

"I think it's supposed to. *Unreal*. It's all so

soothing that you start to lose all your natural precautions. You become strangely…"

"Honest?"

Robin shrugged. "Anyway. Tip number two: don't be afraid to disagree. It's different here—they actually like initiative, most of them. And that's more unreal than the free candy. Three—and this is most important, buddy: don't worry about raises and promotions in your job title. They just happen, like all the other strange and wonderful things around here. The key advancement centers on your housing status. Triple. Double. Single. Extension single. Then…when you've utterly made it…a suite."

From behind, a very small child ran past them toward a thicket of trees, waving two of the free lollipops, both in a bizarre shade of…what? Deep-sea blue? As a mildly exasperated mother came by, giving chase, Robin repeated, "A suite. The sum of all ambition in these parts."

"*Gordon*! If you don't turn right around this instant, I can name a certain young man who's headed for a…*Gordon*! Did you hear me?"

"You can fill everybody's life with perks and rewards," said C. J. pensively. "Make them happy and eager to do well. But some things will not change, right? Parents and kids. The way people get along with each other. Best friends."

"Housemates," Robin suggested.

Gordon's mother came back into view through the trees, dragging an unrepentant Gordon by one hand, still holding the two lollipops.

"One sweet isn't enough?" asked Mother. "Well, you'll go right up to Jeanette and say you're sorry.

And you will certainly give her back her lollipop!"

"I licked them both," said Gordon.

"That's how they type you around here," Robin went on, as she and C. J. watched Gordon and his mom disappear, lollipops and all. "By your rooms. Get into a single as soon as you can. What did they start you in?"

"I've got one roommate."

"A double? That's prime, straight out. Most newbies come in on a triple, which can be gross. Which building?"

"Tower Northeast. It's 16-C."

"Met your roommate yet?"

C. J. shook his head.

"You'll be okay, gay boy. Even a gal with a gray streak can see you're a charmer."

C. J.'s roommate had the rather preppy name of Trent Southy—pronounced *Su¬*-thee—but he was about as far from preppy as an employee of the firm could get. His English was sometimes ungrammatical, his delivery was brusque, and he seemed to have absolutely no sense of etiquette. C. J. eventually learned that there was a lot of that in the firm, following the boss' belief that rough diamonds had the bite to eat into market share, leaving your more traditional country-club suit at an empty table.

Still, rough diamonds aren't generally fun to meet, especially this one. There was a conflict of humors from the first moment, for C. J.'s style was soft and whimsical while Trent found soft men outrageous. He was, at least, tall and very well set up with a slamming physique of the kind that rises from sturdy legs to a heavy upper torso, and if he wasn't conventionally handsome he had a presence. A club-deluxe gay like C. J. had to admit as much. But men like Trent do not make it easy to like them.

"I don't respect initials for names," Trent told C. J. when they shook hands that afternoon in 16-C, Tower Northeast. "What did your father call you?"

"Colin."

"Yeah? So what's wrong with that*? C. J.,* like one of those fuzzy sidekicks in some adventure movie, with stupid jokes when they're running around in the mummy's pyramid. All right, Colin, what section are you in?"

"Marketing."

"What sub? Special Offers?"

"Yes, a matter of fact."

"'As a matter of fact,' huh? You can't just say yes? Same here, anyway."

And with that, Trent abruptly turned and went into his room.

The apartment was nice enough, at least. Very nice, even: roomy and windowed broadly enough to revel in sunlight, it boasted implausibly factory-mint fixtures in bath and kitchen. C. J. kept admiring the way the firm's movers had already deposited his stuff into drawers and closets; he himself never got everything so neatly sorted. It was like

"Don't touch anything in the bathroom that isn't yours," said Trent, looming up in the doorway. He had changed into workout togs and was carrying a little gym bag. "Not anything. *Ever*. You hear? And we'll divide up the fridge so that my things stay mine and...You belong to those little round cartons? This soon? Yogurts, right?"

"Yes. I find it useful to—"

"What kind of dorky food is that, anyway?" said Trent scornfully, as he turned to go. Opening the door, he added, "Food is hamburgers or shrimp cocktail. Candy. Gravy. And you know what I hate? Do you? A soda-pop thief!"

As Trent started out, C. J. quietly replied, "I'll bet that's not all you hate."

Trent stopped short, turned, and came back, letting the door close behind him.

"*What'd you just say*?" he demanded.

Completely unnerved by Trent's angry look, C. J. got out an "I'm sorry." Trent didn't move, so C. J. added, "Forget it. Please."

Trent made the point by staring at C. J. three seconds more. Then he turned again and left the flat.

Well, thought C. J., that is without question the best-looking completely horrible person I have ever met.

Luckily, they didn't see much of each other as the days passed and C. J. got used to the rhythms of life in the firm, because the boss kept everybody busy. Beyond the work day, there were athletic leagues; drama, music, and film groups; a hundred clubs; a thousand meetings. The intramurals confounded genre, as the tennis team stood the stamp club at boat races or the choral society challenged the Chinese-language students to charades.

There was a sound theory behind it: a stimulated

employee community gives of the utmost in inspiration. And this, too: the workers knew everybody slightly and almost no one well. It created a kind of riot of isolation. Even spouses at times felt like competitors in the Darwinian struggle. One of those signs read, GET A GOOD NIGHT'S SLEEP. But another warned, THE BUSY BEE TAKES ALL THE HONEY.

C. J. was eager to take advantage of the social calendar, and he floated from one outfit to another in search of friends of his particular kind. Oddly, they seemed very thin on the ground, as the phrase used to describe it. The few gays he met were all wrong for him in one way or another—and Robin, helpful though she was, knew only *her* kind. Still, C. J. was spending so much of his free time out and about that he and Trent had not had a single "trading views about the world" conversation in their first month together—not that Trent seemed eager to draw C. J. out about anything. They communicated in passing, as when C. J., peering into the fridge, had to ask Trent if he had finished off C. J.'s milk carton, or when Trent, off to the gym again, remarked that at least they both kept their space neat, because he really hated slobs.

In fact, C. J. did not get to see what Trent was like as a social animal till he turned up one Sunday afternoon when C. J. and Robin were passing an hour out by the biggest of the swimming pools. In Speedos and dark glasses, some forty yards off, Trent was joking with and whispering to a very pretty girl in an old-fashioned one-piece.

"That's quite a specimen," said Robin, after C. J. pointed him out. "A build and a half. When the Feds get into secret human cloning experiments, he'll be the first to vanish. Called to the national need."

"He's a mean guy, though."

"Well, he won't get far with Miss Muffett, anyway. She's a virgin to the altar. Christian for sure."

"You know her?" C. J. asked.

"I know the bathing suit. Are you into those big numbers?"

"You mean Trent?" C. J. shrugged. "I didn't used to be. And I wasn't when I first got here. But there's something about all that…that hondo jazz, isn't there? It gets to you after a while. I kind of enjoy watching him modeling in the living room."

"Modeling?"

"Boy, does he love that full-length mirror. Sometimes he'll stand in front of it staring at his reflection as if…"

"There's no vain like a handsome man," Robin put in.

"…as if searching for himself," C. J. concluded.

He and Robin watched as Trent dove effortlessly into the water, surfaced, then tried to coax the girl in after him. He extended a hand to her as if hoping to pull her in.

"He doesn't ever talk about things," C. J. continued. "He just snarls out apartment stuff. 'I owe you a yogurt.' First he was mocking the food I eat, and then…well. But you can't hate a guy with silken skin tone, can you?"

"I could," said Robin, with a wry look.

Now Trent heaved up out of the water and stood before the girl, dripping and marvelous. I dare you not to touch.

"What do you like, anyway?" C. J. asked Robin. "If I'm not prying."

"Besides Candice Bergen? Well, the butch-femme kind of haunts me. You know—stomping and grunting around in public, and then in the sheets…" Robin simulated the shuddering of a frail, with trembly fingers playing air harp. She whispered, "You want to…*what*…to me?"

They laughed.

"Who's your roommate, by the way?" C. J. asked.

"Don't have. They gave me a suite last year."

C. J. whistled. "Madame, it's total!"

"I'll show it to you sometime soon. You'll see—they really know how to turn it on around here. When they like you, I mean. Otherwise…"

Looking up suddenly, Robin led C. J.'s gaze to Trent, who was standing over them, dripping wet.

"You didn't fill me in how connected you are, Colin." Extending his hand to Robin as he introduced himself, Trent added, "Marketing. Special Offers." Then: "Sorry about that," because he had got her hand wet, though he didn't sound sorry, with his dripping muscles and adorably swirled about hair. He did pull the towel from around his neck to dry Robin's hand, with a great show of hetero tenderness. Secretly amused, Robin said nothing, not even in reply to Trent's parting "A pleasure, Ms. Gifford," though she did give him a smile. Adding a nod and "Colin," Trent went back to his lady love.

"What does he want, a date?" Robin asked. "That dope wouldn't know a gal if you gave him a map. He sure is stacked, though. Scope a set of tits on a guy, will ya?" Pausing just long enough, Robin shot a grin at C. J. with "*Colin*?"

The bad sequence began about two weeks after that, when C. J. arrived at his gym locker to change for his workout. Someone had stuck a piece of paper in the draft holes, and when C. J. pulled it out and opened it, he saw a single word, in large computer type in the center of the page:

FAGOT

Crumpling it up, C. J. threw it out and gave it as little thought as possible. He didn't tell anyone, not even Robin. But then came a series of ambiguous incidents—strangers banging into him as they passed in office hallways when there had been plenty of room, an ugly stain on his towel at the pool when he came back from a swim, stares from teams of strangers at the oddest times.

Just…stares.

Then, finally, in the cafeteria one lunchtime, C. J. left his food at the table to say something to his lunch partner, a section co-worker, who was still on line at the cashier. When C. J. got back to their table, he found that someone had poured C. J.'s apple juice all over his plate, soaking his food.

What to do then? Look around, to see who's snickering, nudging companions, guilty? Ignore it, to fight the shame? Leave? C. J. impulsively jumped up, went back to the buffet, grabbed any sandwich, paid for it, and joined his friend back at the table. C. J.

didn't bother to push the tray of ruined food away; it no longer existed. Luckily, C. J.'s lunch partner seemed genuinely oblivious to all this. The pair took their time as they dined, appearing as contented and incurious as oil sheiks at a banquet.

Thinking it over later, C. J. was devastated. He had left his hometown precisely to click RESTART here at the firm, to defeat the unseen enemy of dirty little laughter by leaving it in his dust. But there's always a pack of new haters, isn't there?

Try going to your superiors: won't they hedge and alibi and end in siding with the aggressors? Everyone does; it's easier. That's how the aggressor thrives, whether initiating riots, shouting down political opponents, or wrecking a dinner party with balderdash.

What C. J. did, instead, was to make himself less open to attack by limiting his area of operation. He took lunch at his desk, navigated the halls by falling into step with coworkers, and avoided the public leisure spaces. He spent so much time in the apartment that Trent commented on it, with his usual delicacy.

"Why are you always around, huh?" Trent asked C. J. "Like, what? every minute I'm here. Don't you have, like…"

"What's it to you, anyway?" C. J. calmly replied, at his computer screen.

"What it is, in fact," said Trent, coming into C. J.'s room, "is that I got a promotion today. Deputy head of section, since you ask. And I'll be needing a file from you on your work this last four-week.

Progress and suggestions. All to be summarized, by me, with pages from others, and so on, all very nice and business. Now, a word from our sponsor. I thank you."

"You're drunk," said C. J., not taking his eyes off the screen. He tapped at the keyboard, read, tapped some more.

"I don't never drink," Trent told him while lazily pacing the room. "Pledge to a dying mother."

"Then what makes you so animated all of a sudden?" C. J. tapped a bit more, saying, "You've uttered more sheer English to me in the last minute than—*Hey*!"

Because Trent had put his hand in front of the screen.

"Let's us make a deal with you, Colin," he said, keeping his hand in the way till C. J. sat back in his chair with an air of careless surrender.

Falling heavily into the armchair next to C. J.'s desk, Trent asked him, "You think I'm dumb, right? I'm not, though. Yeah, I look like a musclehead. Sure. But that gets you way in with the chicks. Makes them believe they have the upper hand with a guy, which chicks always secretly want, you know. They think, Oh, the poor thing. Then, ho! Watch me dazzle them with a rhyme poem which I bet *you* think I couldn't hardly invent. Chicks love a cute little haiku, and the next thing after that? Love, true love."

Trent expanded his pronunciation of the last three words as if singing them. Then he grinned. Despite himself, C. J. felt pleasured. It was that singular charm of the big guy who knows he's top. But all C. J. would say was "Haikus don't rhyme."

"Do what?"

"Never…never mind."

"Anyhowsle, Colin." A little bow of the head. "Let's propose a trade with you. Like I say, I'm not dumb. But these reports they want, it's like I could really use a startoff, and you're the man to give it to me."

Trent swung his legs around, resting them over an arm of the chair and stretching out his arms for an elaborate yawn. Then he said, "So how I see it is, I'll help you so you'll help me."

"You'll help me with what?"

"What do you need?"

"Nothing."

Trent looked at C. J. for a bit, then slowly shook his head. "Everybody needs something, Colin. And I need help from you in organizing these reports, because I'm, like, not the world's champ at organizing a writing. Spell check? Got it on, bro. But what about smart check? Coordination check?"

"You don't have to give me anything," said C. J. "I'll help you and we'll call it even."

Trent thought it over, with his head cocked. "Okay, chief," he replied, rising to his feet with a grunt. "I'll owe you one. First report's due a week from Monday. Can you get me in shape by then?"

"Easily. One thing, though—if you suddenly blaze forth as a master of English prose, they'll be suspicious. You need to start out merely competent and then improve till each report is a zinger. They'll call you in and ask what gives. You produce a *How To Write* handbook with plenty of dog-ears and highlighting. And, for that touch of initiative…marginal notes."

Trent wandered through the room some more. Then: "You really know stuff, huh?"

C. J. nodded, swiveling around in his chair to watch Trent, dressed to captivate in cutoffs and a mesh tank top.

"So what's this handbook?" Trent asked, coming to a stop beside the desk. Placing his hand atop C. J.'s head, he said, "Show me on the screen."

C. J. paused, enjoying the feel of Trent touching him: something intimate from someone so distant. They say it was like that in the Old Days, when you'd get an unsigned mash note from a coworker and have no idea who had sent it. Turning to the computer as Trent took back his hand, C. J. clicked onto Amazon for a manual. "Style and clarity," he said, scrolling and clicking. "Think of the office as a video game and the book as your strategy guide…Ha! *This* one!"

Things went well between C. J. and Trent after that. The big guy remained a lout, suspicious of novelty and disinclined to change his mind about anything no matter how wrong he might be. Still, he appreciated C. J.'s sacrifice in time and concentration in helping Trent on his office reports. Better, the boss liked what Trent was doing. His third report was *very* commended.

That was the day C. J. found a live mouse in one of his desk drawers. It startled him motionless, as the mouse, strangely unaware, kept harmlessly plugging along the path it had chosen for itself amid C. J.'s colored paper clips and post-it pads. Closing the drawer, C. J. emailed the office manager to effect a cleanup of his desk and quit for the day. "Personal emergency."

Could this be a crazy accident or more harassment? Had his unknown pursuers, defeated by the change in C. J.'s schedule, taken all this time to arrange another strike on him?

"What are you doing home so early?" asked Trent, as C. J. walked in.

"Do you really care?"

"I'm deputy head of section, aren't I?"

C. J. halted and tried a glare. It had no effect, so: "I'm not in the mood for another of your—"

"Don't you mouth off at me, Colin! *Hey*! Where do you think you're—"

"Let go of me!"

Pulling C. J. around to face him, Trent said, "Don't you fucking dare show me your back when I'm—"

"I don't work for you, Trent!" cried C. J., shaking Trent off and backing away from him. Trent followed. "And what are *you* doing home, while we're at it?"

"I got a gold star on my book report."

"Right, your office report that *I helped you on*? Because this is how you thank me?"

"I was trying to before you started fucking around with me!" Trent grabbed C. J.'s arm again. "*Huh*?" he emphasized.

"How…about…letting…go of me?"

"Put a please on it first!"

"Not to you!"

As if it had all been a merry stunt, Trent released C. J., throwing his hands up with "I swear I'm true blue, Professor Colin of the manners squad here!"

Heading for his room, C. J. stopped, turned to Trent, and said, angrily measuring out his words, "You know what, Trent?" But then he gave up. He just went limp and started back to his room. "Forget it," C. J. told him.

"Actually," said Trent, following C. J., "what I wanted to tell you, Professor Colin…Lookit, are you listening to me?"

"No," said C. J., opening his closet.

Trent slapped the side of C. J.'s head—lightly, just enough to annoy.

"Cut it!"

"Now you're listening. Yeah, and you dislike me even more than usual, right?"

"I don't dislike you usually," said C. J., getting out pajamas and bathrobe.

"Oh, I'd a-said you do, mostlies. And others do, too. Dislike me. Hey, he's so noisy and full of himself, right? A boxer in the ring. Pounding at you, sweating."

C. J. turned down the bedclothes, laying out his pajamas.

"Now, some chicks will quite simply hate me about it, so it's cute when they learn to like me, after all. You sleep in pajamas, Colin? In the day?"

"I thought I'd take a nap," said Colin. "So, if you don't mind…"

"I do mind. Since I been thinking along certain lines here. Such as what happens to me if my man Colin stops helping me with my office reports? Am I gonna be worse off, when the, like, entire quality of my writing goes clunkorama? Could that be a plan of Colin's, now?"

Colin just looked at him.

"How about an answer there, Mr. Fixit?"

"You think I'd…You're actually accusing me of—"

"I'm only asking, man. Christ, why do you fucking fight with me every little—"

"Leave me alone, Trent!"

Furious, Trent grabbed C. J., who immediately began to struggle, crying, "You stop right now! You *stop*! Let go and…" Still struggling but silent now, C. J. gradually wound down, still in Trent's grasp, shaking his head and panting. "I can't…" C. J. got out at last. "Because I can't…"

Trent let go of him, and C. J. retreated, reaching the bed and absent-mindedly picking up the pajama top. "I want to take an afternoon nap," he said. "Yes, whether you like it or not. So how about getting out of my room?"

After a moment, Trent came up to C. J., took the clothing from him, and dropped it on the bed.

"This isn't like you, son," Trent told him. "Sure, I have shoving matches all the time. Like, hooray, it's time for another. But you don't never have them, so tell me what's wrong. And a nap? At your age, that's like saying you want to be dead. Lie down there, go silent, wait for nothing. What's that about, huh? I was going to talk office reports with you, which, like, I need your help again, but that'll wait. Just you now tell me what's wrong."

"Nothing's wrong."

Trent half-smiled and smoothed out C. J.'s hair.

"Colin, I can make you tell me if I want to, and there's fucking not a thing you can do to stop me. But ho, man. Maybe I can help. You're helping me, right? Just tell Uncle Trent now. Is it office stuff? The boss?"

C. J. picked up the pajama top and bottom, saying, "I don't want to talk about it," but Trent once again tossed them away. Adding the robe to the pile, he sat on the edge of the bed, taking C. J. down to sit in front of him, hemmed in by Trent's legs. Holding C. J. with an arm around his torso, Trent said, "Don't make me hurt you, Colin."

"It's not about the office," said C. J., trying to concentrate on how badly he felt but distracted, lulled, by proximity to Trent. "It's nothing you need to know."

"You'll talk now, I say."

Trent tightened his grip on C. J., using his free hand to take hold of C. J.'s forehead. It was unpleasant rather than painful.

"Stop, Trent. Please?" C. J. put a pleading hand on Trent's arm, to no effect. "It's not office stuff, okay, but I'll tell you, all right?"

"Start now."

"I'm being hounded by bad guys. They…they do things to me and I don't know who they are."

Trent took his hand off C. J.'s head and loosened his grip across C. J.'s chest. "What do they do?" he asked.

C. J. told him everything, from "Fagot" to the mouse in his desk.

"Faggot misspelled, huh?" said Trent. "An imperious clue!"

"That's a misuse of the word 'imperious,' which really—"

"The culprits have to be in section, right? Or they

wouldn't have access to your desk like that." Patting C. J.'s stomach—apparently the signal to get up—Trent rose, taking C. J. with him by holding his sides till they were both on their feet.

"Could the mouse have been an accident?" C. J. asked.

"In this sterilized police state? They must have gone to the next county to find a mouse the fuck at all."

Funny, wasn't it? No "So you're a fag, huh?" from Trent. No "You're gay?" He seemed only to see a problem that called for a solution. Picking up the pajamas to look them over as if he'd never seen a pair, Trent said, "I can take care of this, Colin. I think I even know who might be behind it. This place is so damnitall happy that the stupids don't have any way to let loose. Some guys just need to be stirring up trouble for someone. They yearn to be riled up. If not the pay, then the chow. If not the…who the heck knows? The fucking chess club. Or some guy's different from me. Hey, Joe. Bill. Carstairs. The other stupids. Some guy's different from us, let's get him. Huh, Colin?"

C. J. didn't say anything. He watched Trent press the pajama top against himself in C. J.'s mirror, moving the arms around. Posing. Holding his chin as if he were Rodin's *The Thinker*. Waving hello at distant friends.

"See, I could have sworn you were holding out on me on an office thing," Trent went on. "It's why I was so interested. I been hearing certain rumors."

"About what?"

"You. Anyway, we'll leave this to me. Just go around like normal. Show yourself all over the place, and if it happens again, you come straight to me, understand?" Trent turned to C. J., the pajama top seeming almost to shiver in his grip as he let it down. "Only it *won't* happen again. That I fucking promise."

C. J. then said, "I'm sorry we fought just now." It was not the first time that he aimed to effect a peace by apologizing to the belligerent.

"Yeah? So how about letting me try on these pajamas? I always wondered how they work. Okay with you?"

"They'll run small on you."

"Just to get the idea of them, because they look so intelligent, you know? Smart people put them on and get ahead in life. Yeah, I always knew there was a trick to it."

For some reason, Trent decided to use the mirror in his room, and C. J. dutifully trailed him there. It was a little nicer than C. J.'s. The firm designed the multi-person flats with adjoining good and better rooms, to promote competition, and Trent's boasted one wall of shelving separated by a mirror than stretched from floor to ceiling. It was very nearly a movie set. As C. J. hung around trying to look helpful rather than mesmerized, Trent stripped and pulled on the pajama pants.

"What's this string?" he asked.

"You tie it up like a belt. Then, if you tug on the bow, the bottoms just fall."

"That'll be cute with the chicks. 'Hey, darlin', what's your name, now? Clothilde? Why, that's so sweet that I hear music in it, and perhaps would sing of—Ho! Who dropped my pants down through no fault of mine?"

Trent let off a guffaw and C. J. tried to join in.

"Now the top, as we unfold it. Real fresh, I see. Virgin, huh, Colin? It's college suave in every fine white button there." Putting it on, leaving it unbuttoned, running a hand over the material with a gentle humming sound, Trent at his ease.

"It's so smooth feeling," he said. "Like kissing up for sex. And the top hangs over the pants is my guess."

Trent admired himself in the mirror.

"What do you say, Colin? The young executive? He relaxes by candlelight, reading love poetry to my sweet Clothilde, who is swept away. She can't resist to feel his muscles through the…what is it now, cashmere?"

"Cotton."

"He says, 'I could show you the ink on my shoulder caps, only then I'd have to kill you.' Hell, let's show her, anyway."

Grinning like a dancer in a sex club, Trent pulled the right front half of the coat back, then the left. Listening to a beat on his head, his knees bent, he swiveled down, shaking off the pajama top altogether, then addressed the mirror.

"'It's like so, Clothilde. You and me have it going, and you know to which I may refer. Am I going to be nice to you, Clothilde? Well, that depends on you, my sweet.'"

This is the fourth time, C. J. was thinking, his dick hard against his pants as he turned away from Trent and walked through the room a bit. I'm in love again, and I'm not going to be able to do anything about it as long as I'm living in this apartment.

"'Say what, Clothilde? What's that, now,

sweetheart?'" Lazily tracing the contours of his physique with one hand, he took on a mock-ironic tone while waving a finger of the other hand at the mirror. "You say all the guys you know are made of sugar and spice? So now you want to taste a real guy and see what that's like? You want sex on Mars, Clothilde?"

Fascinated by the way Trent was examining his chest muscles, C. J. failed to notice that Trent had given up his vignette with Clothilde and was using the mirror to look at C. J. Catching his eye, Trent took hold of the drawstring about his waist and pulled. The pants dropped to the floor, bunching up momentarily as they slid past Trent's half-hardon. Not unpleasantly, Trent said, "Want to cocksuck me, gayboy?"

C. J. stared at Trent, then shook his head no.

"Sure?"

"I'll just," C. J. started to say, but it came out hoarse and he gave it up. Without looking at Trent, C. J. got the pajama suit together to go back to his room, but Trent stopped him with a hand on his shoulder.

"I'll take care of that problem for you, Colin, true enough. You can trust me to the bank on it, son."

C. J. paused, wondering why he didn't just fall to his knees and get on Trent's dick. Just do it, he told himself. What are you waiting for, they used to say, an engraved invitation? But he forced himself to turn away and went into his room. And they said no more about it.

It took a few weeks, but C. J. finally told Robin what had happened. Almost all of it.

"Man, that is one sensualized dude" was Robin's

view of it. "If he was a gal, he could be Miss Bergen herself. I don't care for the excessive force in the scene, but you boys of the posse do like your business rough. You think he'll come through about the harassment?"

"If anyone can, I guess. He has incredible resolve. One of those ruthlessly accomplishing guys, and I have to admire that. They always seem to…they get what they want from life, don't they?"

"But why did he think you had office news? So much intel flies around this campus, you never know if there's any substance to it. Could they be offering you a promo? So soon?"

"Not that I'm aware of."

Robin thought it over. "Want to come up to my place? It's time you saw a suite."

It wasn't the flat itself, though it was lavish: sitting room and "media center" beside the standard kit, along with the firm's patented space-age featurettes, including a one-stop laundry that ran itself, from wash to dry.

And it wasn't the way Robin had personalized it, not least with a ton of photos on the grand piano.

"This is like 1952," said C. J., scoping the pictures the way one reads through the menu of a gourmet restaurant. "Who are all these wonderful people?"

"Family."

"Siblings?" C. J. liked looking at other people's family pictures; someone once told him it was his nicest quality. "Cousins and such?"

"Everyone."

"And a grand piano. I should have learned, I'll bet."

"It's a max social tool. Years ago, they sold lessons that way. Like, you sit down and play the Best Song Oscar and take over the party. Strictly a guy thing, of course, because it's chicks who respond to music when a male's in charge. Hetero chicks. No true gal ever fell for art, if I can share another secret of the trade. And it's my misfortune, because I do have the gift."

Knowing that C. J. was about to invite her to play, she waved him away and said, "No, come with me instead—something I need to show you."

Robin led C. J. into a small room off the media center, furnished with nothing but a desk and a computer terminal.

"Tap in," she said. "First your section. Now search 'Events.'"

C. J. did as told, and a long menu of clickworthy entries materialized, under options from "Leisure" and "Church" to "Health" and "Eros." Each offered data on what C. J. had been up to lately, complete with video life captures.

"You couldn't cut into this on your home screen," Robin told him. "It's stat-restricted to the boss and suite-holders."

C. J. now searched Trent's name and did a little spying under "Health." There was a site count on Trent's pool and gym history, right down to the machines he used at what weight.

"Shocked, right?" said Robin, looking over C. J.'s shoulder. "But there's no personal stuff. One tiny viol of privacy, and Human Resources would get on you like the fold on the wolf. All you can view is public events, same as they have on video cameras all over cities now. Everywhere, young man. With tape and Google, there's no such thing as a secret any more. But you can see the boss' angle—he wants his promos to know what's happening in our world, from the pools to the Hoedown Club. What the new talent is up to, size 'em up. Initiative? Smarts? If they've got quality, it'll show up in everything they do. Tap yourself in again, but this time…No, go ahead."

C. J. went back to his data, searching the heading that Robin pointed at: "Echelon."

"That screen," she directed. "Click there."

And that's how C. J. learned that he was on a five-list for a suite.

"Tower One," C. J. read out.

"What number are you?" Robin asked. "On the list."

C. J. said nothing.

"Tell me, big boy. Read a girl the script."

C. J. was thinking about this.

"Yep," she went on. "You have made it in your, what? late twenties? Suites generally go to thirty-somethings, or at least those with a long history here. What have you been up to be so favored, hey?"

Staring at the screen, C. J. got out a bit about his programs and billing rates. Robin looked on as he checked to see if Trent was up for a suite as well, perhaps in the same tower.

Trent was not up for a suite.

"You can't bring your roommate along, can you?" C. J. asked.

"Nope. And you can't turn down a suite if they offer it, either. Not if you wish to prosper hereabouts."

C. J. nodded. Turning back to the screen, he clicked some more, bringing forth shots of Trent: in the office, on the grounds, charming a damsel poolside.

C. J. let out a long breath and said, almost in a whisper, "Will you just look at that beautiful monster?"

Lightly petting C. J.'s shoulder, Robin said, "You left something out of the story, didn't you, pal?"

More or less at that moment, unbeknown to C. J. and Robin, Trent himself was in a meeting with his superiors—yes, on a Saturday. It seems that questions had arisen about the order of names in the five-list for the next suite. An emergency of sorts. All the concerned section heads and their deputies had been summoned, and, when C. J.'s name came up, Trent spoke for the first time, and at length.

After noting C. J.'s abilities, Trent proceeded to take his candidacy apart. C. J., he explained, was—these are the words he used—"emotional" and "unstable." He relied too much on instincts and hunches and not enough on hard market data. True, his guesses could prove spectacularly successful, or why was he on the five-list at all? Still. C. J., Trent claimed, dealt in luck practice, in sorcery. "Witchmaking" was the word Trent used, a coining all his own—and he reminded those present of a recent catastrophe in which a business launched a line of lifesaving drugs in uniform packaging, without the size and color variations that strengthen I. D. security. Staff at a prominent hospital had confused doses because of the look-alike presentation and nearly killed a few patients, including the relative of a celebrity. The tabloids had kept the news in cycle for a week, and why? "Witchmaking," Trent repeated. "Flying without instruments." Then, with the tiniest wink of an eye: "Litigation to follow."

Of course, none of what Trent said about C. J. was true. Further, office politics shake a rich cocktail of envy, challenge, and sheer bloody *No you won't because I'm here, too!* Trent's head of section, who had nominated C. J. in the first place, countered Trent, defending C. J.'s candidacy with stinging power.

Trent sat through it with his company-player smile fixed in place while touring about with his private demons. That busy little C. J., huh? Picked his allies just fine, right, such as helping that big stupid Trent with his pathetic paper work that makes him so proud. Earns him respect from the high and mighties running around the place. Muscle-trash Trent! Then watch that C. J. sneak away to a suite as Trent crashes without the C.J. word skills. No loyalty to that kid, no stuff, no just-plain-to-heck fuck!

His face unreadable to the others, Trent took part in the show-of hands vote and bustled off at the adjournment. A suite, huh? Yeah, and we're gonna see about that!

C. J. was in his room by then, composing a letter to Trent, to take up this very matter of the suite. C. J. planned to summarize what he termed his "interaction" with Trent—C. J. avoided the word "relationship" as presumptuous—and explain how he felt about the possibility of moving out.

It was a fearsome job, because everything C. J. wanted to say was forbidden. He has learned about the blade of honesty, how it turns against you all too often. Truthtellers go around wrecking lives. People avoid them, especially people like Trent. What mistakes we can make with them!—as for instance when C. J. told Trent that no one was harassing him any more.

Trent looking at him with an indecipherable expression. "Well, I found about it, didn't I?" Trent told him. "Like I knew I would."

"Who was it?" C. J. had asked.

Trent separating laundry in his room, piles on the bed, a year's supply of Speedos. "Don't even bother, Colin" was his answer. "Don't waste time with that kind. They'll never get it."

Trent turning from his clothes on the bed, facing C. J., shirtless Trent.

"They're never smart. They never listen to anything. They miss out on promotions, they get asked to leave, and nobody knew they were even here. On the planet earth."

Trent whistled once, short and shrill, timed to a jerking of his right hand, whisking clean.

"Yes, but..." C. J. couldn't let it go. "What did you do to get them to stop?"

"I told them what I'd do to them if they bothered you again."

C. J. was going to extend his hand for a shake, but Trent had turned back to his laundry. To his back, C. J. mouthed, "I love you."

And Trent stopped what he was doing. Without turning around, once again, as if he knew C. J. so well he didn't even have to hear words to know what he meant, Trent asked, "What did you just say?"

"I didn't say anything" was C. J.'s reply. After a bit, he went back to his room.

And now, constructing his letter, he struggled over how much he could put into words. He set it down that men like Trent get taken for granted as little more than models, even when, like Trent, they have hidden resources. He told Trent how much he liked living with him, how…fond of him he was.

That word! Fond: mawkish and pathetic, as dainty as a new saint's first postcard home. Worse, C. J. closed by saying that he felt so honored to know a man like Trent that he was torn in half about the suite. C. J. left it to Trent to decide whether C. J. would take the promotion or not. Whatever Trent decreed, C. J. would accept.

He left it for Trent to decide! How was C. J. feeling then? Such a submissive—a hungry—act! Virtually exulting in this ceding of power, C. J. sent the email to Trent's terminal and headed off to a meeting of the German Cinema Club for a screening of and coffee-table aftertalk on Fritz Lang's *Metropolis*.

Trent was putting the same time to wicked use, brooding and smarting over his failure to keep C. J. from being offered the suite. Trent had not only lost the vote over C. J.'s promotion: his was the only nay. That kind of thing never looks good, and it has an odd way of turning up in your personality file in suggestively euphemistic phrases of disapproval.

After working off some of his anger in a super-session at the gym, Trent tried to arrange for a hookup at the pool. Yet he worked at it like a dilettante, posing and faking and barking up the wrong trees. But then, he wasn't engaged in hooking up just now; he was in a mood to Settle the Score with Colin, using those words over and over in his head as the evening darkened and the pool closed and the traffic along the campus pathways thinned to stragglers and dog walkers. Yes, and to Trent, striding along now here, now there, deep in the splendor of his rage and just this side of muttering and furtive movements. Sooner or later we all reach this level, reveling in our martyred virtue, letting the wheels turn as we go over every last bit of the treachery to which we have been treated. Yeah, the big dumb guy Settles the Score with you, Colin, you…conniving little…*adviser*. Winning the vote for a suite and probably packing right this very minute as we speak.

He sounds drunk. But Trent really didn't drink, ever, as he has said. By the time he got back to the apartment, it was late enough for our fine little Colin to be asleep. Likes to get his beauty rest with an early to bed, doesn't he? Yeah, and the place was dark, giving Trent the satisfaction of banging around blindly, to disturb C. J. His door was half closed and his light out, the usual sign that he had retired. He was afraid of the dark, so he slept with a bit of hall light shining in. Take some dark on me, Colin, Trent thought, shutting the hall light off.

After stripping for bed, Trent grabbed the top of the bedclothes and drew them back savagely, as if sheets and blanket could raise yet more noise in the flat. He suddenly went all still, listening for a response from C. J. Perhaps a sigh of resignation: poor Colin, with his oh, just *unbearable* roughneck roommate. No response. And then Trent thought of a thing to do. He went into C. J.'s room, pulled the covers down, grabbed C. J.'s feet, and swung him around so that he was on his back with his legs on the floor. Then Trent leaned over in the darkness, pinning C. J.'s arms to gaze down at him from real close. If C. J. has been sleeping, he sure wasn't sleeping now.

"Hello there, Colin," said Trent, quietly.

C. J., motionless, didn't answer.

"If you shout, do you know what I'll do to you?"

"I won't shout."

"I'll tear you apart like a paper doll."

"I won't shout."

Still holding C. J. fast, Trent climbed onto the bed to straddle him. They were motionless and silent for a bit. Then Trent said, "If you're so clever at everything, how come you're down there and I'm up here? Huh, Colin? Wearing those stupid lullaby clothes again, too?"

With that, Trent ripped the pajama top open and planted a thick angry kiss on C. J.'s lips.

"It's all from this beauty contest they hold in South America somewhere," Trent told C. J. "Private clubs. First it's the boring part, where the girls sing Broadway hymns and want world peace. Then it's the sex part. The judges taste the girls' skin, to see if it's just right. Up and down them, long as they please. They suck on the girls' tits with the slow deep pull that hottens them up. Catch on to it, Colin?"

Pausing in his report, Trent brushed C. J.'s hair off his forehead, then went on with "Yeah, they eat those girls up, and the juices run free as the crowd goes wild. They feel the girls' tightness. What an extravaganza, huh? You won't see this at any sports bar, son."

Moving his hands to C. J.'s neck, Trent got so close to him their noses touched.

"Who's your daddy?" he said. "Who's your daddy, Colin boy?"

Pulling C. J. up, Trent flipped him onto his stomach, yanked the pajama bottoms off him, and worked C. J.'s arms and torso till the top was off as well. Then Trent pushed a finger into C. J., who now made his first attempt to escape. Trent gripped him, C. J. struggled, and Trent then threw his body weight onto the younger man, grabbing C. J.'s head with both hands to warn him, "Give me a reason to smash you up, you traitor, now!"

C. J. went still. Trent went back to task, taking his time loosening C. J. up till Trent could slip two fingers in and rub them against each other.

"They call that the cricket," said Trent, "which you probably know all about it. Do you like my style, or do you think the boss does it better?"

After a few moments of that, Trent said, "I think you're ready now." Moving off C. J., Trent told him to get up, and C. J. turned over, staring at Trent without attempting to rise. Strangely enough, Trent now extended a hand to C. J., who hesitated till Trent said, "Take it. You're going to do this voluntary."

C. J. did what he was told to do, and Trent took him to his own room. Slamming the door, he turned to

C. J. with a look of immense resolve. But C. J. had a plan now: he took a step toward Trent with his palms up, in non-aggressive mode.

"Trent, you're right about everything," C. J. quickly got out. "I screwed up, okay, but give me a chance and—"

"Stop being nice to me," Trent told him, pushing C. J. to sprawl on the bed. C. J. leaped up again, but Trent grabbed him, shoved him back down, and made his preparations so hastily that he was on his way to the center of C. J. before either of them was ready for it. Licking C. J.'s ear, Trent whispered, "When did you know?" as he moved inside him, not roughly. "When did you know, Colin, huh?" And "Tell me or I'll hurt you just exact the way you're going to hurt me."

"I can't hurt you," C. J. got out as Trent reared back, flipped C. J. over, and got inside him again with "Everybody likes you, huh?" Moving more rapidly now, Trent seized one of C. J.'s hands, pulled it up to touch Trent's right cheek and then pressed it against Trent's chest—his heart, really. "But who do you like, Colin? Do you like me like this?" Dredging kisses from C. J.'s mouth, Trent ordered him, "Hold on to me." When C. J. hesitated, Trent barked, "Do it now!" just like the step-class teacher in C. J.'s Tuesday evening gym program. Grapevine, kicksaw, do it now!

"Why do you have to be like that, Colin?" Trent suddenly cried, to which C. J. answered, "Is it because of my letter?"

Still partnering C. J., Trent stared down at him uncomprehendingly. Yet he had heard enough to gasp, "*What letter?*"

And just then C. J. gave off a wail of startled

delight and began to let loose. Inspired by the sight and knowing that it happened only because the boy was entirely his now, Trent pulled out, tore off the rubber, and shot off himself, with a hoarse shout of "*Here goes nothing*!"

Now down to the stillness, the panting, and neither of them knows who has the next line in the scene. Having fallen back on the bed next to C. J., Trent managed to utter the words "I gotta go home" while C. J. turned to look at him.

"Was it my letter, Trent?" he asked once more. "Did I say too much truth about love?"

"I gotta go home," Trent repeated, feeling for C. J. with a stray hand: his wet hair, his waist. Trent let his hand rest on C. J.'s stomach, saying it one last time. I gotta go home.

After a very long time, then, Trent heaved himself up in a bound. "You stay right there," he told C. J., as he started off toward his shelf space. But then Trent stopped, turned back to C. J., and said, "Don't move, don't go anywhere in the world."

C. J. looked at Trent, then replied, "Okay."

"You answer 'Yes, sir' to me."

"Why should I, though?"

"Because I told you."

C. J. now said, "Yes, sir" so ungrudgingly that Trent softened despite himself. Crossing to the shelves, he got a towel and went back to C. J. to dry his hair and skin. Then Trent wrapped the towel around his middle, pulled the blanket back to cover C. J., and went to the computer terminal to wake it up and read C. J.'s letter. Now and again, he turned to look at C. J., his expression unfathomable. When Trent had finished reading, he thought for a bit, reread the entire letter, then got up and got his bathrobe. At the bed, he pulled C. J. up and onto his feet and wrapped the robe around him. Then he brought C. J. to the desk and sat him in the chair as if showing him the email.

"I know about this already," C. J. told him.

Without answering, Trent pulled up another chair, reversed it to sit with his chest against the back, and began:

"When I was in high school, we had an activity very popular with the oldest kids. Seniors only was the rule. An old tradition or some such, nobody ever told a grownup about it. We called it Scorning. And what it was, you would pick out someone in the school. Juniors were the idea, but anyone. Maybe a few sophomores. And the deal was, for the whole year you would insult this guy all the time. Crush him down every chance, no rules. No limits to it. But only in public, see? If it was the two of you alone, you'd just be wasting it. Is that true?"

Trent paused, waiting for C. J. to respond.

"Yes, sir," said C. J. at last.

"No, you say, 'That is true.'"

"That is true."

"Scorning. Right. Which I never knew why it was so popular, or why some victim didn't go to the…well, not the principal, now. He just wants to shuffle papers and have committees. But somebody should have…Anyway. I never took part in Scorning, which you had to be pretty major to get away with that. See, if you didn't choose your victim and scorn him, the whole everybody else would go after you. The whole kaboodle of them, scorning *you*. Because if you get away with I won't, then Jim will, and Marilee, and like that. One guy says no and gets away with it, the whole thing falls apart, doesn't it? So the bad guys, which they never run out of no matter where you go…the bad guys have to po-*leece* the ranks, yes indeedy. Like the cowards who moused your desk. Am I right?"

"You are right."

"But I'm a big talent in the place, it so happens, because of some nifty little quarterbacking on the football squad. Plus I am a big physical type, and your typical little bully is afraid of me, as you maybe noticed. It's freedom insurance. Everyone leaves you alone to your pursuit of happiness. But there's this thing I know, which I knew it from the day you joined up here—that if you and me were back in school like that one, then I would've picked you out for Scorning."

"Why, Trent?"

"Because."

Trent rose and dragged his chair up to C. J.'s so close that when he sat again C. J. could hear him breathing.

"But I don't like Scorning," Trent went on. "So it's a puzzle to me, though I know I feel better when for instance like I make it hot and fearful for those junkheads who were hounding you. I took care of them, all right. But now this other thing. See, we…we held a meeting about the suite list today. And I fought against you, Colin. I undervalued your work and your character. I lied, is what. And that was because I had to stop you. I *have* to, Colin, because…'cause why did they put you in with me? If the boss knows everything…Yes, but…Like I could have told them about you being hounded. Let them draw the obvious conclusion and then no suite for Colin. But I didn't tell them. I didn't go there at all. You know why?"

"Because that would be Scorning."

"Yes, Colin. That would be Scorning. And now…see…" Trent took C. J.'s hands and pressed them together inside his own, and Trent smiled. "Now I read this letter from you here. What's it about, I wonder, with taken for granted and hidden resources?"

Trent rubbed C. J.'s hands a bit, then laid them carefully on the back of his chair, his hands resting upon them.

"And he is fond, our Colin. He would be a fond boy now, and lets me decide does he take the suite or not. Do you by any fucking chance know what it means to get a suite around here? And yet you would let me…Do you take my fact?"

"I take your fact."

"Yes, and I said I'd've Scorned you. I didn't today, but back then…No, delete that. I tell you to *turn down the suite* and you will *turn it down*?"

"Yes, sir."

Silent, Trent stared at C. J. Then Trent asked, at once beguiled and disbelieving, "Why would you do that for me?"

C. J. replied, "That I cannot tell you."

"Oh, Colin. I can make you tell me."

"No, you can't, Trent," said C. J., gently. "That you can't."

He felt his face get hot and weepy—*damn*!—as Trent got up, turned his chair around, and sat back down.

"You'll be staying here with me," Trent told C. J.

"The invite to suite will come in late tomorrow morning, and at lunch you'll come back here and I'll stand watching while you turn the suite down. Don't tell them you can't afford it, because they always raise you to equalize the rent hike. Just say 'regretful personal reasons.'"

Reaching for C. J., Trent pulled him into his lap and whispered, "Remember, I'll be inches away, Colin, my boy. And I'll know what you do."

C. J. lightly rubbed Trent's left arm. "Okay," C. J. said.

"'Yes, sir,'" Trent corrected, but in an uninterested tone, heedless of whether or not C. J. would respond. Trent even repeated "Yes, sir" as if punctuating rather than expressing anything, and gripped C. J. possessively. He has the right.

"Yes, sir," Trent said again, feeling the tears as they ran down C. J.'s cheek. "Boy, do I love it when they cry."

THE FOOD OF LOVE

"Cruise alert. Man with white labs."

"Too skinny."

"Not skinny," said Ken. "Slim and way romantic. Look at how his pooches rub against his legs to show their devotion."

Davey-Boy snorted—ironically, I think—as Ken offered me a taste of his jam. He takes it neat, spooned up right out of the jar.

"Those dogs didn't choose him, like at your gay bar," said Davey-Boy. "Your Splash or G. They're just being affectionate so he'll upgrade them from kibble to spaghetti and meatballs."

This is one of those summer afternoons in Central Park. We were scarfing up the last of a picnic on a bench near the southwest entrance that West Siders use by the flock, letting it all happen around us, as befits a slow and easy Sunday. As the time drifted by, we inspected and remarked on the talent, an *American Idol* based on looks. The man with the labs passed quite close to us as he headed for Central Park West, his animals cascading around him. Now they were sniffing, now alerting at the pigeons, now frantically trying to get to another canine, this one a collie padding along with great dignity behind a mother and a stroller.

I asked, "Why do dogs act as though the mere sight of another dog is the event of a lifetime? What are they so excited about?"

"Too skinny," Davey-Boy repeated, as he watched the man and his labs pass out of the park.

Think of those fantasy tales in which the protagonist is granted the gift of invisibility. I felt like him, because when you pal around with Chelsea Boys no one knows you're there. Ken, my cousin, is a maximum leader of Chelsea culture. But Davey-Boy, the greatest rejection machine in the chronicle of gay, is a big showoff to boot. Just now he was wearing Lederhosen with suspenders and no top.

"Twink alert," Davey-Boy murmured, eying two of the genre, approaching from the north in warm conversation. Ken's spoon rattled along the sides of the jam jar as he sought out the last bits.

"Aren't you worried about antagonizing your waistline?" I asked him.

"I'll just gym it off with extra program tomorrow."

"'And another thing,'" Davey-Boy put in, as he imagined the conversation of the two young men he had just indicated, using a Valley Girl accent and a tone of martyred righteousness. "'I'll thank you to *entirely* stop *making*, like, just a *total* mockery of Scott's *eating habits*. Just because he's a vegan—'"

Changing voices, Davey-Boy interrupted himself with "'I *only* pointed out that if he keeps ingesting

Tofurkey he'll, like, maybe start to *look like one*!'"

"'Oh, and *you* don't have flaws? Such as crowding the bathroom with more *toiletries* than the *Taj Mahal*?'"

"They don't look like they're fighting, though," I said.

Suddenly, one of them turned to the other and struck his cheek, hard and loud. Many of those around us missed it, but a good two dozen or so stared.

Davey-Boy chuckled. "Twinks make terrible boy friends," he observed, as the guy who was struck stalked off and the other one looked after him angrily.

Licking around the inside of the jar top, Ken asked, "Why do twinks make terrible boy friends?"

Davey-Boy shrugged. "Because they're twinks." Getting up and stretching ecstatically to show off his torso, he added, "What's next, my boys?"

Next for me was a mass tea with my English friend Ian. Back in London, and sometimes in New York, Ian is theatrical, so the guest list favored stage people, including one ex-friend of mine. The parting embittered him (though he was the one who ended the relationship), and I did my best to avoid a confrontation. This unfortunately landed me in the clutches of a woman who wanted to recount the fabulously pointless saga of the long lost videotapes of some old television show. I kept trying to prompt her to the finale.

"And they were in the trunk in that closet?" I prayed aloud.

"Yes, but first comes the wonderful surprise!" she merrily warned me, preparing to launch the next hundred thrill-laden episodes.

Then someone called out, "Bud!" and I was saved—by another ex-friend, my old actor pal Alex. This parting wasn't bitter, just one of those show-biz things. They go Hollywood, or they join boutique cults and pretend to be straight, or they *are* straight and get married. Then you fortuitously cross paths and you're best friends all over again.

I really like Alex. By this time he was nearly Of a Certain Age, but he took care of himself and had grown into his looks: as a solidly-built, masculine forty-something. Many a soft guy dreamed of being plundered by Alex some startling Saturday night, and Alex encouraged the fantasy; he liked being cast in studly roles, and if you know actors I don't have to tell you that they are never not auditioning. Yet Alex had a secret soft side. He fought it, mind you. He was forever invigorating himself in the mirror, developing rufftuff facial expressions and stances. He would gesture like a halfback. He growled. And, of course, as an actor he had the skills set to see the transformation through.

"Why are you here?" I asked him, as we edged our way into the other room after a sequence of glad reunion noises.

"I came with the Bryan-Browns," he explained, referring to a Broadway PR outfit. "I'm in the new McNally, and they're handling it."

Congratulations, shaking hands again, Alex taking it in manly stride. Cut to:

"I'm not speaking to you." This came from Anne Kaufman Schneider, ensconced in an armchair in a corner. She's George S. Kaufman's daughter, known to supporters as "Kiss of the Schneider Woman."

"Now what?" I asked her.

"I lent you my private CDs of James Lipton running through that *Sherry*! score," she said. Anne doesn't much like musicals based, like this one, on her father's plays. When he signed it, with Moss Hart, it was *The Man Who Came To Dinner* and it had only one song in it, which is about as musical as George S. Kaufman liked to get.

"I returned those CDs," I told her. "I gave them back to you at Kitty's, last Christmas. That Boxing Day party."

"That's why I'm not speaking to you," she said.

Joke. So we sat next to Anne, and I introduced Alex, and we played urban smartiboots and started dishing various Broadway types and were having a fine time when my bitter ex-friend appeared, making a beeline for Anne.

"Here it comes," I murmured to Alex. He was puzzled but clearly aware that we were in for a touch of geschrei.

Treating me to a look of pure gargoyle, my ex-friend said, with what was supposed to be a tone of crushing disdain, "Hello…*Ethan*!"

Then he turned the faucet of love, delight, and merriment upon Anne, no doubt to demonstrate to me what heights of friendship I was missing out on.

Fine, fine. Alex shot me a quizzical look as my ex-friend made his exit, but Anne is her father's daughter: the offspring of the master of wisecrack would have the line and the timing all set. She waited three beats, then turned to me with "I want the story and I want it now."

In the end, Alex and I decided to play catch-up, so we repaired to my place for what John Rechy (I think) referred to as "coffee and." En route, Alex got very curious about the encounter with my ex-friend, finally getting to "Was it…intimate?"

"Good grief, no. He's just mad at me. Permanently."

"Huh," he grunted, all jaw and profile. "Relationships," he added. "It's total war." Now he shakes his head with handsome rue. "Everyone thinks, if only the sex part will work. But the sex part is a cinch. It's the emo, right? Feelings. They're so…everywhere a lot." He gazes about as we walk along Fifty-Third Street. Alex ponders the world. "Mad, you say. But how mad? Irritated? *Enraged*? Or just…disappointed? There's rather a lot of that, I have to say—guys not getting what they want and holding you responsible."

"You know," I told him, "you're speaking more slowly than you used to. It's a little like taking enunciation class from the football coach."

"Yeah," he agreed, as vaguely as possible. "The *coach*."

"It casts a spell, though," I admitted. "Are you working up a playing profile for the McNally? Or will you go through life like this?"

"If only guys weren't so intense, you know. So touchy if you don't give them enough attention and the like." Deftly stepping around a street crazy with a rapt expression and the hair of a Morlock, Alex asked, "Do you still live with…"

I nodded.

Smiling, Alex said, "I remember how he does

cute things. What do *you* guys do about emotions?"

"We don't have any. He's the houseboy."

Alex suddenly jolted to a stop as we reached Madison. "Are we walking?" he asked. "All the way?" He gestured at the road, a long sweeping motion of his arm, capped by a sudden closing of a fist. "Like it's medieval and there are no wheels?"

"Alex," I told him, "stop acting."

I was fumbling with the keys at my door when it swung open a crack to disclose Cosgrove's sock puppet, Baron Portugee. In a foreign accent of some vampire kind, the puppet introduced himself and invited us to join him in ze Casbah—but when I pushed the door back and Cosgrove saw Alex, he and the Baron went quite, quite still. I have to admit, if you're into first impressions, Alex gives a great one. Tall and handsome: accept no substitutes.

"This is Alex, from way back, in case you don't remember," I said as we passed inside and dropped stuff on the couch. Well, Alex did; actors always have those stupid bags, in case they run into Florenz Ziegfeld and have to present a résumé.

Music was playing: Cosgrove had been investigating the closet where I retire LPs, and now celebrated a passion for Jane Morgan, who was just polishing off "Can't Help Lovin' Dat Man."

"Hey, the same old place," said Alex, browsing a bookcase as one might in a Roundabout "once over lightly" revival of some thirties boulevard comedy: looking without seeing.

"You're indicating," I said, pulling him around so that he faced into the room. "Name one book title you just read and I'll treat you to dinner."

He laughed. "It's the old Manhattan stee-ory," he said. "Living quarters. The things we love arranged around us. Wish I had my own place. One night of solitude, it's all I ask…What?"

This was directed at Cosgrove, who was still at the door, staring at Alex. Finally coming to, Cosgrove pulled off the sock puppet and approached Alex while I went into the kitchen to pour the sparkling.

"If you're an actor," I heard Cosgrove ask, "where's your class?"

"About twenty blocks to the southwest. Every Thursday afternoon."

I heard the music go off, and Cosgrove asking, "Do you do improvs?"

"Often."

"I go to an improv class myself, but it's more about psychodrama, which is how you would use acting to work out your personal problems. We don't do scenes of Shakespeare and such. Sometimes I appear as the international café society parasite Baron Portugee."

"I thought that was your puppet," Alex was asking, as I returned with the sparkling. "Are you both Baron Portugee?"

"'There is only one,'" Cosgrove explained darkly. I think that's from *The Exorcist*.

Handing Alex his water, I asked, "Do you still live in that crazy sublet?"

Carefully flashing a half-smile, Alex nodded. "Sigh," he said.

Alex resides in a problem palace, with an ever-changing ensemble cast. There are three bedrooms, but at various times as many as five or six people have fielded the rent. Of course, there's always one who's not tidy and one who's too tidy and one who eats your corn flakes. At one point, everyone in the place was a hunk actor like Alex; visiting was like walking onto the set of an orgy video.

"It's pretty orderly now," Alex was saying. "Darielle has the lease, and there's only me and her boy friend. Neil. Older guy, sort of bald. Gray, even. Incredible body for an oldster, all-day gym stuff."

A sip of sparkling. Alex and I were on the couch, Cosgrove sitting on the carpet in front of us.

"Yes, he…he doesn't work, Neil. Darielle's ee-made it, financially, you know. All controlled, the lady executive. She can afford anything she needs, so she's got freedom. Marriage? Kids?" Alex grunted. "No way, my lady. She likes her sex steady, and Neil…" Now he plays it admiringly, with a touch of wonder. Poster blurb: "A finely nuanced portrayal"—the *New York Times*. "Yeah, the same old story. Neil's got a big one. I mean, *really* big. So Darielle…so she…" More sparkling. "Well, she made the deal she wanted, didn't she?"

"How do you know he has a big one?" Cosgrove asked.

There was an abrupt silence.

"You should try sitting in on Cosgrove's improv group," I suggested, coming to the rescue. "They really do address their personal problems in a constructive way—*and* it's acting."

"It's dangerous theatre," Cosgrove remarked.

"Yes," I said, "it can get quite dire when somebody starts acting his guts out. I often expect the drama police to barge in with weapons drawn. 'Step away from Patti LuPone…'"

"You're in the class?" Alex asked me.

"As a spectator."

While Alex demonstrated concern—head a-tilt, eyes down, thinking privately—I asked Cosgrove to rustle us up some dinner, and he went off to design salad platters.

"If the eats are piled in an artistic way," he said, heading for the kitchen, "they call it 'boy food.' Because all the sous-chefs are cute gay guys."

Alex was intrigued when I told him that Cosgrove had taken up fancy cooking.

"See, that is what I call controlling your life," he said, as the reassuring clamor of crockery and utensils pealed out from the other room. "Because Neil earns his pay not only for sex. He runs the household, and that means the food, and it's…it's like everything is grilled chicken and veg. And don't you hate your chicken grilled? I like chicken burgers with surprise flavors. Oh, and wait for it…" Buoying himself up with a guzzle of sparkling, Alex went on, "He stands over you and forces you to partake, like…you know, daddy when you wouldn't eat your runny eggs."

Cosgrove popped out for "He should try tiny chicken filets in lemon-honey-ginger batter, which I serve with potato heads and a very strict green salad." Then he went back to work.

"Potato heads?" Alex echoed, longingly.

"French fries, except round," I told him.

Lowering his voice, Alex asked, "Didn't that fellow used to be, like, a demented waif?"

I lowered my voice, too, just for fun. "Remember

my buddy Dennis Savage? He's been mentoring Cosgrove in—"

"Ha!" cried Cosgrove, coming back among us while drying his hands on a towel. "But now he's on the enemies list!" I guess our undertone needs work. "I asked so nicely for the recipe to his hundred-tastes meatloaf, and what did he do? I ask you!"

After a bit, Alex replied, in John Wayne's voice, "Okay, pilgrim…what?"

Suddenly dropping the Dennis Savage feud thing, Cosgrove said to Alex, "At parties, do the ladies line up in front of you in wedding gowns?"

Alex shot me a look, meaning "Translation, please."

"Cosgrove thinks you're straight," I said, "so don't lots of women try to land you?"

"Hmm," Alex answered. "The explanation, yes." Letting down his voice to the depth of a prizefighter's, Alex told Cosgrove, "I'm as gay as you are."

"You'd be a hit at my improv class," said Cosgrove. "Tom-Tom acts out his office headaches, but I present little epics. Some nights, we have a skit with Napoleon, Socrates, Jessica Dragonette. All the greats. You could be anyone you want."

Then he went back to salad making.

Alex nodded, but he didn't say anything for a while. Finally: "You're in charge of him, of course. Right?"

"I pay his bills, if that's what you mean."

"*Ha*! If only! Darielle pays Neil's bills, but he orders us both around as if…and she doesn't mind, because that only proves how hung he is. You know his take on relationships?" Moving close for a confidence, Alex said, "He tells me, 'This is the way it works—one is the boss and the other one isn't.' So…are you the boss?"

Before I could respond, Cosgrove came back in with "And if that Dennis Savage shows up, you tell him I said this kitchen is ¬*sealed to him*! Now we'll see!"

And back into the kitchen he went.

"Yeah," Alex went on, in a slightly dreamy tone. "Darielle? A newspaper junky, *total*-lee. Like fur in Alaska. After the dinner coffee, she likes to read from the editorials to me, then discuss. Not Neil, though. He's in there watching some basketball game. But after a while he appears in the doorway in just running shorts and that idiotic T he likes, all cut up for summer comfort. There's almost none of it left except a rectangle under his chest. Though, one must admit, he's quite…And he says to her, 'Come to daddy.' Holds out his hand, so completely in charge."

Alex demonstrated, waggling the fingers of his right hand.

"Says, 'Come to daddy, now.' Can you imagine?"

Cosgrove was back. "Does Dorian come to him then?" he asked.

"Darielle. Yes, she…*Oh*, yes. Leaves the newspapers on the table-o, and goes right…She travels a lot. Because of her job? And when she's away I ask Neil not to cook for me, but he insists."

"Can't you just tell him no?" I asked.

"Well, but then he puts his hands on your shoulders and fixes you with those pushy gray eyes. And you…you…" After sputtering a bit, Alex gave up, thoughtfully watching as Cosgrove left us again.

"You can lose your way sometimes," Alex finally said. "So it's nice to be looked after. Independence gets so exhausting."

"What's your new play like?" I asked, briskly moving us on. So we started in on that. Those of my readers who know actors will have heard this speech, because it's always the same. The author's a Shakespeare, the director is Max Reinhardt, and the other actors are the Moscow Art Players. Two weeks later, ask about any one of them, and the answer is invariably, "That cunt."

Meanwhile, Cosgrove was serving the salad plates, with fresh-parsley butter sauce on the baguettes we get at Gourmet Garage. They're the authentic kind that stale in a day, and they're why we live in New York.

In fact, Alex asked about the bread, in case he could persuade Neil to stock it, too. So we were back to Neil—a subject that so obsessed Alex it felt a little like taking tea with Captain Ahab.

Baron Portugee noticed it too. "Alex is soft on daddy," said the sock.

Alex has a masterly wink, and he treated us to it now. "You want the story?" he said. "Sure, we're fucking."

Uh-oh: the heavy stuff. Cosgrove relinquished the sock—"No, no, I want to hear!" the Baron cried—as Alex went on, "You know how it is, when…God, what are these little things with the shiitakes?"

"Polenta sticks," Cosgrove replied. "Now start dishing."

"Right. I told you how Darielle's always on the road. Or actually it's airplanes. As if she can't stand, you know, communal…Are there any more polenta sticks?"

Cosgrove took Alex's plate and went into the kitchen, to Alex's "Ah, thank you, my man." Alex in his collegiate voice: crewing on the Schuylkill. And "That is *so* conducive," he added, when Cosgrove returned with seconds.

Alex polentaed for a while then decided to eulogize the butter sauce. "Do you feed like this all the time?" he asked. "Because someone has to go to a lot of work…" Licking his slice of bread, he added, "Spices and herbs and…"

"This isn't the eating scene from *Tom Jones*, okay?" I said. "I want the story and I want it now."

Alex went on munching a bit, then let it out: "One of those New York surprises, you know. Last Halloween. I was in that…you remember, that eerie thing set in Renaissance Florence. Codpieces and tights." He shuddered for us. "I mean, I like to show off as much as anyone, but give me a mesh T any day. Anyway. You recall that play, yes?"

"All male cast," I murmured, recalling the code words with which early Stonewall porn movies addressed their audience and which adequately described Alex's Italian play.

"Yes, heavy on skin, wasn't it?" He chortled at the memory. He didn't laugh. He didn't giggle. He didn't chuckle. He *chortled*. "I was friendly with the costume guy, and he let me walk out of the theatre on the last night in my full kit." Turning to me, he said, "You didn't by any chance…"

"No, but I heard."

To Cosgrove, Alex explained, "The top was a

half-coat, with bare midriff. The pants divided at the crotch with a lace-up fly-ez-vous kind of thing that never quite pulled the two halves together, if you can conceive. And of course no undershorts, because they didn't *have* undershorts in Renaissance Florence. Yes, and so out you go on stage and the entire audience immediately stares down at your junk. You can see the heads bobbing."

Catching up on his feed, Alex noted, between bites, "If you could just…market these…these polenta sticks…like fast food, you know…you'd make a fortune. It's a nosh and a half."

"They'd cost too much" is all Cosgrove had to say about it.

Finally Alex got to the heart of the story. "The Halloween party, now. Neil is usually so busy at the gym evenings that…well, suddenly he was there while I was getting ready for the party. Of course, he thinks it should be illegal to dress so…openly, I guess. Like all sex maniacs, he's got a puritan front. Except when he's stroking himself while he talks to you, which he does all the time."

More eating.

Then: "What do you call this saucy bit with the--"

"Get," I told him. "To. The. Plot."

"Bud," he said, smiling, "you haven't changed at all."

"You have," I answered. "You're a walking rogue's gallery, toying with various superhunk identities as you decide which one suits the successful actor-about-town. And I thoroughly approve. It's gay life: you invent yourself."

"Man, these polenta sticks!" he cried. "I ate them

all till nothing's left!"

Expectant silence from the rest of us.

"Oh, right. So Neil was there when I got back from…and, yes, I was drunk. *And* Neil followed me to my room, watching me undress. Ho, watching? Running his pickpocket fingers along the laces at my dick on those, what? Casanova pantaloons, saying, 'Did you score chicks?' and 'You don't need to tell a man with sand what "actress" means.' He got right into the shower with me, too—or was I even going to take one? Right in the water with me to say, 'She's in Houston.'"

Nodding at us.

"Darielle. Sure. You were wondering, right?"

A sip of sparkling.

"*And* he's soaping me up in that owning way of his, and of course the muttering. He's a great one for those menacing undertones, our Neil is. Like 'Think you're so high and mighty.' Or 'Teach you to mind your Ps and Qs.' Kind of shoving me around sort of thing. Toweling me off very roughly. He loves to be rough. It's not a pose, though. A *pose* it is *not*. It's just…how he's made. Want my plate now?"

Alex extended it to Cosgrove. Using the French bread, our guest had cleaned the porcelain like a Westinghouse. Taking it, and mine, and piling them onto his, Cosgrove told him, "Don't say any more till I get back." He deposited them in the kitchen and rejoined us in perhaps three-and-a-half seconds.

"You like a good story, huh?" said Alex. "Do you enjoy it when a big winning guy like me suffers a takedown?"

No—and, anyway, is this Alex's story or Neil's?

Because why are those heteros so obsessed with cock that they have to come play big shot in *our* house? And Alex really does make a tempting picture. His dentist strokes his hair, can't help himself.

"Well. So Neil puts me to bed—you know, that 'poor guy's so drunk I'll have to take care of this myself' routine. And he left me there, but then he came back with the sex fixings and went right to it. No cocksucking or anything. Just…'Knees up to the ears, now' and 'Pull you down to me for all-the-way, so take a deep breath.'"

Cosgrove's blurb was ready: "'Husband by day, hustler by night,'" and I put in, "'Come to daddy.'"

"He talks all the way through it, too." Sip of sparkling, build suspense. "Like, 'There's but one way to teach a sarcastic intellectual like you.' He words you up. But he won't play me the music. His oh so private audiotapes. See, when he and Darielle are together, I can hear a concert through the door—drums and flutes, some mid-Eastern concoction. And mixed in the tape is some dirty talk and…chanting or something. One voice keeps saying, 'Honey and figs, what a sexiful treat.'"

"What?" I said.

Alex nodded. "Over and over. 'Honey and figs'—is that some catchphrase in, like, Beirut? And another voice says, "Do it, do it, do it." Two beats. Then he went into a quiet half-singing tone: "Do it, do it, do it." And then he winked at us: a nice one, slow and studly.

"Will you stop?" I said, though I was enjoying it, too.

Cosgrove said, "I would prefer a medley of Kander and Ebb showstoppers."

"Why doesn't he play the tapes for you?" I asked.

Alex shrugged. "Couldn't say, old man."

"Is he nice to you?" Cosgrove asked.

"'We'll soon see how high and mighty you are with your plays and books stuff, when you sigh for me like a chick.'" And, no, he isn't nice to me. He's rough with me. I call him 'Captain.'"

"Why?"

"I don't know." Now Alex is charmingly helpless in his all the same man-of-the-world way. "Commandingly rueful"—*New York* magazine. "Who can explain what happens to you? Maybe he puts something in the grilled chicken. He sits me in front of him on the edge of the bed, playing with my ears—ha, you like that bit? 'I'm going to turn you inside out and seal it with a kiss.' And this is said," Alex added, leaning in for a confidence, "in the low tones of a liar of the night."

"Is that from some play?" I asked.

"Is it weird? Yes, it's…sex is weird, why doesn't everybody know that? And, yes, I struggle—because you were wondering, right? But he holds me fast. He—"

"You're a big boy," I said. "You can shake him off."

"Yes," with a hand on my shoulder. He plays the friend, understanding and forgiving. "But do we want to shake them off?"

Cosgrove asked, "Except does he like it when you call him 'Captain?'" while Alex finished off his sparkling.

"He doesn't like or dislike. He's just gruff and hung as he goes through life. And that unbelievable physique along with him."

"Does Dannylynn suspect anything between you two?"

"Or would she care, Darielle?" Now he's grinning in a sort of *Private Lives* put on. Alex did the play once, somewhere in the midwest, and the critics complained that his shoulders were too big for Noël Coward. "She knows her man. If it keeps him home instead of out looking for…" He almost absently extended his glass to Cosgrove, who refilled it so fast he passed himself on the way back from the kitchen. "But what if I can apply this someday to my work? One of my long ago acting teachers used to say that everything that could possibly happen to you is in some play sooner or later. You use it all."

Now he polished off the water and rose.

"Thank you for dinner, and—no, don't get up." Of course, we did, anyway. At the door, he said, "I need to come over again and have some more polenta sticks, because the best friends want us happy."

Some people wait for you to open the door, but actors know how to crack a Segal lock (bottom left, top right), from always making exits. Alex treated us to another wink and vanished.

Boy. How do you come down from that? Luckily, we were distracted by the return of Dino Croc, who had been on a play date with his current boy friend, the schnauzer on the ninth floor, Robespierre. Dutifully frolicking a bit around Cosgrove, the dog then got to the serious business of seeing about dinner.

"You can tell why he's an actor," Cosgrove was saying of Alex, while serving Dino Croc's Salisbury steak and mashed, which he likes fridge-cold, with just a hint of tomato sauce on the meat. "What is his type, would you say?"

"He's a Heavy Father. One of the last of the kind, perhaps." At Cosgrove's wondering expression, I went on, "From the days of melodrama. Tall as a rule, and somewhere between matinée idol and villain. Stylish and courtly but with a dangerous undertext."

"Who is he the father of?"

"Usually an unmarried young mother during a blizzard. He's the guy at the door pointing at the weather and crying, 'Thou art no daughter of mine, thou rebellious and sinful jade! Go—and never darken my doorway again!"

"Yes," Cosgrove agreed, "with that authority physique." He cut and washed a stalk of celery for Dino Croc, who likes to top off his meal with roughage. Starting on the dinner dishes as the dog tucked in, Cosgrove asked, "How come he lives in a crazy house and doesn't have a romance with someone regular instead of Donniemarie's daddy?"

"Darielle. But Alex has romances. He just isn't clear on his role yet."

He sure was clear on those polenta sticks, though. Nothing would serve but that Neil abandon the grilled chicken and take up the cooking of polenta sticks. Cosgrove was happy to share the recipe—"unlike certain neighbors I could mention," he added darkly, looking up in the direction of Dennis Savage's apartment. But, we soon learned, Neil claimed they were too hard to master, and then he got even by making chile with hot Mexican ingesta and made Alex match him spoon for spoon. And Neil, Alex told us, can eat anything.

It was such a baffling tale, though, with more holes in the plot than *Heaven's Gate*. Every time Alex visited, I found myself playing editor. "Why," I began, on one of these occasions—but Alex waved me off with "He was shirtless in suspenders and…" Then he made a resigned gesture. Why? Gay life is why.

"But isn't he bald?" I asked.

Exasperated, Alex replied, "God said, 'I'm going to take your hair away, but first I'm going to give you the biggest dick in history, even flaccid. You want clipped or unclipped?'"

"Did the lady eat the hot chile?" Cosgrove asked.

"*Darielle*, everybody, and no. She's on the model's diet. Coffee and cigarettes three times a day."

It has become a rule, on Alex's now frequent visits, that Cosgrove give him a doggie bag of polenta sticks, complete with a little plastic pod of mushroom sauce. Alex told us he has to sneak them in and hide them or Neil would gobble them up.

And Neil this and Neil that. Isn't it odd how guys like Alex never realize how utterly *gone* they get? How confessional? One time, he reported, Darielle left on another trip, and, a mere ten minutes later, Neil grabbed Alex and said, "I need my back rubbed nice, and if you cooperate instead of giving me guff I won't rough you tonight."

"Are you complaining," I asked, "or bragging?"

"Why is your dog looking at me like that?"

I sighed. "I could explain how he wants you in the other chair so he can teethe on your shoelaces and pull them open, but I don't want any distraction from the driveline. Which is: are you glad about Neil or sad about Neil?"

"I'm collecting material on Neil. Think you're the only writer-a-go-go around here? Always fancied getting out my own story or two. I'm going to exploit Neil's Farmer Haystack rap. 'I'll straighten out your antennas.' Or when he won't let me sleep the night with him, he disdains it with 'With your head on my chest? That's the womenfolk's delight.' Cosgrove has invited me to his next improv class. As guest artiste. Do you think? I'm inclined to, frankly."

"That'll make a nice episode," I said. "So far this whole story has been nothing but a living room."

He nodded and then drained his sparkling in a final sort of way.

The rules governing Cosgrove's improv class are Byzantine, and they keep changing. When Davey-Boy joined, he persuaded the others to elect a "director" to oversee the doings—a violation of the very meaning of improvisation. Further, although it was Davey-Boy's intention to be elected director-for-life, like a third-world despot, the job rotates from meeting to meeting.

On the day Alex came to class, Tom-Tom was the director, and, to Davey-Boy's annoyance, Tom-Tom kept consulting with me before each act (or whatever they should be called). I never take part in the proceedings, but I pay for the pizzas we order at the start of the session, so everybody likes me.

A typical evening: sketches on the latest romantic snafu, the "in-laws" (meaning your boy friend's social circle, which as a rule hates you and seeks always to turn him against you), miseries on the job. Volunteers play the other characters, but, because they're all making it up as they go, events can take unexpected turns. For example, Cosgrove was supposed to be somebody's devious attorney, but instead he turned into an old vaudevillian reviving his art, which consisted entirely of a performance of the old hit-parade number "If I Knew You Were Comin' I'd've Baked a Cake."

Then Alex took a turn. When he asked for one assistant to play opposite, a storm of hands went up; word had got out that Alex is officially single. The chosen one was Korby, a nice-looking kid who always smiles at the pizza slices but noshes on his own black sushi tray. Tom-Tom set the two players on chairs about five feet from each other, warning them not to rise until "the key moment," whatever that turned out to be. Then Davey-Boy, next to me in the back row, piped up with a reminder that newbies have to enact a scenario dictated by the group. It's like improv cabarets of the 1970s, when the comics would let audience members choose the program—*Pinocchio*, say, presented in segments in the styles of Shakespeare, Chekhof, and Rodgers and Hammerstein. Yes, they had to make up the songs, too.

Tom-Tom rejected all suggestions as banal till Davey-Boy called out, "Let the big guy be a New York City police detective. He's going to arrest Korby for soliciting, though they never spoke about money."

"Then I'm innocent," Korby snapped back, carefully addressing Tom-Tom. Everyone's afraid of Davey-Boy.

"Yeah, you're innocent," snarled Alex, in a heavy working-class New York accent. "Bust you for that gay stuff, and I'm even queerer than the rest. I could go for a lad like you, after we terminate that music playing at night, which disturbs my rest."

"What music?" asked Korby, confused.

Davey-Boy said, "Just go with it."

Catching on, sort of, Korby said, "My parents let us play CDs for lullabies in bed."

"You're not doing little folks' sleepy time now, though," said Alex, tugging on his tie, opening it, pulling off. "Are you, youngster?"

Korby looked at Alex for a moment, then turned to Tom-Tom. "Where is this, though?" Korby asked. "And do I get an accent, too?"

The baffled Tom-Tom started to answer, but Alex, losing the New Yorkese, cut in with "I told you how it is with Darielle and me. She pays the bills, is it? But how is she in charge when I'm the one with the dick?"

Opening his shirt cuffs in silence, Alex now got topless, and Korby suddenly stood up.

"No standing yet," Tom-Tom reminded him.

"The one with the dick," Alex repeated, as Korby sat back down. "And since you're always serving me up helpings of guff, looks like I got to give you an attitude adjustment. You'll see who's in charge right about now, I'd say."

I have to admit, the class definitely seemed to prefer this segment to Cosgrove's séances and Tom-Tom's office melodramas. The pizza munching that habitually punctuated the entertainment had come to a halt.

"There's but one way to reform a busy little glamour boy," Alex went on, still seated but now turned to face Korby. "And that's with cock up the ass, rough as she goes."

Alex suddenly yanked his belt back, opened his pants, pulled out Thumper, and started working himself.

His eyes wide, Korby asked, of anyone, "Is that the rules?"

Next to me, Davey-Boy murmured, "Head for the hills, young Korby."

Hard as stone in little more than the time it takes to sneeze, Alex got out of his shoes and socks with the practice of the pro that he is, edged his trousers and shorts down, and then abandoned the chair for, yes, the key moment. You know how they speak of somebody's jaw dropping? You haven't seen what that looks like, but I have, and it was Korby just then.

"Come to daddy," Alex told him.

Korby didn't move, and Alex went for him, inspiring Korby to leap to his feet and get behind his chair. I got up, too, for I was Alex's sponsor and I felt responsible. But Davey-Boy rose with me and put a hand on my shoulder, saying, "Don't worry." Oh, yeah? How does he know not to worry? Alex lazily thrust Korby's chair away and took the boy in his arms, running a hand through Korby's hair. I heard gasps from the audience, I think. Then Alex turned Korby around to hold him from behind, and you could tell that Korby was hard, too.

"See?" said Davey-Boy, as we sat. "Korby likes it crazy."

"And you know that how?" I asked, getting as response one of Davey-Boy's bland "Why should I tell you?" looks.

"Going to teach you respect," Alex was saying as his fingers traced the contours of Korby's face. "When I'm through laying you, I'll feed you my spunk fresh from the cock. And you will take it to the last drop if you know what's good for you."

"I won't," Korby replied, though I dare say his tone lacked resolve.

"My, but yes," Alex insisted, his voice growing soft with, I guess, his own worried recollection. "You got to, now, or didn't we both know sparks were flying between us from the first minute?" Alex was running his right hand over Korby, feeling him through his clothes, pulling at them, the shirt up above the beltline now to press skin, holding the boy close with his left hand. It was the perfect actors' scene: no director needed. Even the audience was superfluous.

"And didn't you tantalize me," Alex went on, as Korby kept moving his head around to gaze up at him, "with that all-day tick-tock of being so nice to look at and talk to, ekcetera? A tasty dish like you? Huh? Didn't you? Huh? Huh? Huh? Huh?," grabbing Korby ever more tightly at each *Huh* till their heads were at even height and Alex, out of words, swayed with the boy on the verge of something, like a drunk captivated with the memory of once having been coherent.

"Come to daddy," whispered Davey-Boy, next to me. He seemed as captivated as everyone else in the class. The truest top man is the one who can pronounce those words with confidence, don't you think? That's what I call *acting*.

Then Alex straightened up and looked at us all, and Korby turned, put his arms around Alex, and held on. Korby doesn't care—or know—what this is about.

He hasn't heard of the demanding older guy in Alex's apartment, of the bartending and unemployment lines that interfere with your living, of the roles Alex plays. Korby just likes Alex; everybody does. A handsome man will save you from ekcetera.

"It's a role in your life," Alex suddenly announced, absently stroking Korby's hair. "And he can't take anything away from you."

"As the lights fade on that touching scene," cried Tom-Tom, jumping up to start the applause. It was the biggest I ever heard in the class, almost an ovation. "*Merci, vachement*, to guest Alex and the faithful Korby, though I wonder what happened to the police detective doing an arrest. Now, who else wants to improv?"

Nobody moved, perhaps especially the two actors on stage. Korby clung to Alex, occasionally perfecting his grip as if trying to climb inside him.

"I'll give him credit for the fancy rap," Davey-Boy told me. "But what an exhibitionist."

"Look who's talking," I replied. Davey-Boy was in a stoker's white mesh top and jeans with most of the buttons missing.

The stillness of the scene was finally broken when Alex gently disengaged himself from Korby saying, "Thank you for your support." You know, as in Best Supporting Boyhunk. Korby hovered as Alex picked up his clothes and then came down to Davey-Boy and me. Those in the audience turned to their neighbors to launch the ritual gay critique of the performance while reengaging with their pizza slices. Some remembered to hand their crusts to Tom-Tom, who regards them as a delicacy.

Cosgrove came over, too, to pat Alex on the head, a strangely endearing gesture, especially as Alex has a good six inches over Cosgrove in height.

"Aren't you going to get dressed?" Cosgrove asked Alex.

He wasn't, it seemed. Sinking into a chair, he concentrated on looking drained and distant.

"At least put on a sombrero," I suggested.

In reply, Alex winked. Not the most secure or reassuring of winks, however. Not a facetious wink.

Cosgrove murmured, "'Lucy, you got some 'splainin' to do.'"

Now Korby drifted up to tell us how awesome it had been, and Alex started putting his clothes on, slowly, then faster, then fast enough to challenge time travel. This is what comes of those quick changes behind the scenes.

Looping his tie, Alex told Korby (and very casually, this, almost as if uninterested in what the reply might be), "I'd like for us to get acquainted. You got a place, youngster?"

Korby nodded, and off they went—no, first I stopped Alex to inquire just what that scene was about. He laughed, resting his right hand on Korby's right shoulder with such tender authority that the boy shivered. Come to daddy.

"Why ask?" Alex said to me. "Lookers get their way, that's all."

And *then* off they went.

Teetering on his chair with a wicked smile, Davey-Boy asked the question of the day: "So…was it real or an act?"

No one responded. Around us, the room was very

gradually emptying as the guys finished off the pizza, put heads together, cleaned up the space under Tom-Tom's fastidious leadership (in French), and departed. Cosgrove, putting some chairs in order, quietly but repeatedly sang the first strophe of "If I Knew You Were Comin' I'd've Baked a Cake."

Then I answered Davey-Boy's question. "We'll find out if it was real or an act after Alex's play opens and he makes an appearance in my apartment to explain what was happening."

"And you would know that how?"

"These stories always end that way," I said.

Alex's play got raves and the entire troupe was cheered, so he was dropping in and dinner-partying all over town, to enjoy being as doted upon as a newborn Italian male. He even made a date with Cosgrove to learn the recipe for polenta sticks by watching over the maestro's shoulder. Cosgrove shooed me out of the kitchen so I wouldn't distract with show-biz kibitzing.

Just as well: because Dennis Savage's reading lamp died of old age and he didn't feel he could tackle Bed, Bath and Beyond singlehanded. So I rode shotgun.

We have an outlet nearby, an odd place: vast yet filled with all the stuff you're never glad to buy. For instance, a bathmat instead of the piano selection of some obscure English musical of the 1930s.

Dennis Savage is no connoisseur of reading lamps. He chose the first one he saw and we were back on the street in a moment. On the way home, he announced that he was going to give Cosgrove the blueprint for that meatloaf after all—but when we got home, Baron Portugee roiled out of the kitchen (followed by Alex with a plate of polenta sticks, but Alex doesn't do much in this scene).

"*Go*!" cried the Baron, at Dennis Savage. "And never darken my towels again!"

"He's going to give you that recipe," I put in.

Cosgrove hesitated. But the Baron would not be soothed. "*Ha*!" he retorted.

"Very well," said Dennis Savage, picking up the box of lamp. "I think I'll just lock up that recipe in a galaxy far, far away."

Infuriated, Cosgrove followed him as he headed for the door, both he and the Baron imitating Dennis Savage's walk. But suddenly Dennis Savage put down the lamp and, without turning, quietly asked, "Are you animating that stupid puppet behind my back?"

Cosgrove said nothing, and when Dennis Savage whirled around to surprise him in mid-puppetry, the Baron was not to be seen.

"I'll give you the recipe," said Dennis Savage, "if you give me the puppet."

"*What* puppet?" asked Cosgrove, defiantly.

I told Alex we'd best sit and watch the show. Laying down the polenta sticks, he said, "You guys should put in a popcorn stand."

"Show me your hands," Dennis Savage told Cosgrove.

Keeping his puppeted right hand behind his back, Cosgrove slowly produced the left one.

"The other hand, too," Dennis Savage ordered.

Cosgrove slowly withdrew his left hand, transferred the puppet behind his back, and now extended the empty right one.

"No, both hands at once," Dennis Savage insisted.

Cosgrove very, very slowly deposited the puppet in the waistband of the rear of his trousers, and produced both his hands at once. The encounter had taken on the feeling of a duel to the death by Kabuki samurai. With an *adagio* that would have had Tim Conway's slow-moving-old-man portrayal gasping in awe, Dennis Savage tried to circle around Cosgrove while Cosgrove matched him step for step, always keeping Baron Portugee hidden from view.

It was Dennis Savage who lost the war of nerves. "*Give me that puppet*!" he cried, throwing himself upon Cosgrove and seizing the baron. "*Yes*!" he called out, giving the baron a victory shake. "*Now*!" he added. And "*See*?" he triumphed. (So to say.)

"But the other player," Alex noticed, denoting Cosgrove, "is impassive. Enigmatic, you see? We are left wondering where his dramatic arc will take him."

Indeed, Cosgrove waited quietly, his features expressionless, as Dennis Savage took a folded-up scrip out of his pocket and gave it to Cosgrove with "Here. And that's the end of the puppet show."

"Young Cosgrove seems to have lost," Alex went on, as Cosgrove opened the paper to be sure it was the longed-for recipe. He momentarily gazed up at Dennis Savage, who just stood there holding the puppet—the sock, really, for the days of Baron Portugee had surely come to an end.

"He *seems* to," Alex continued, gorging on those polenta sticks. "But he got what none of us ever has enough of."

I made a guess: "The trade of something

worthless for something he needs?"

"The passionate attention of an interesting man."

Parking himself next to us on the couch, Cosgrove began reading as he muttered, "Little does he know that I have another puppet just like it in my dresser." Now in a suspicious tone, he said, "Wait a minute—did you leave something out? Where's the turmeric?"

"There isn't any," said Dennis Savage, retrieving his lamp after stuffing the baron into his pocket.

"The whole town knows you put turmeric in everything!"

Well, Dennis Savage took his lamp upstairs, Dino Croc returned from another play date, and Cosgrove decided to test drive the meat loaf model and went off to the market. Alex and I fed the last of the polenta sticks to a grateful Dino Croc, who then went into the bedroom to see about a nap. So Alex and I were alone. And he began:

"Some years ago, when I was still a young 'un, I worked out of state with one of those veterans who'd done every classic in the canon and shared the stage with many a name. You and the other startingouters go out drinking with him, and he tosses all his stories at you. He told us about a job he had, opposite an actress of great respect. Yes, you would know her, Bud. Crazy, of course—all the great ones are. I hope to be crazy one day. But deep and searching, too, this dame*aroo* of the stage. No jargon on this lady—never uttered word one about 'finding my cadence' and all that amateur twaddle. But—the old veteran told us—she had this sort of fabulousness quirk, that she never finished rehearsing. Just kept on working on her role right through the run. The show might freeze, but she never did.

"And the old actor hated her. Because he had finished his character prep, and the blocking, and whatnot. Games with props. An almost undetectable limp. Learned his lines. He had *done* his *work*, is how he put it. Yes, but playing with her…well, he never knew what she'd be up to next, did he? She didn't miss cues or change lines, no. Still. Once she got into a scene, you had absotot alutely no goddamn warning of how she was going to play it. Because her character would mesmerize her. Turn her inside out. She couldn't resist it. It was a case of…in his words, this is, now…'Needing the knowledge.' You *need the knowledge*. Because it makes you smart and new. Makes you young. That's why I did that improv, by the way."

He got up.

"I needed the knowledge," he repeated. "How it feels to…"

"How'd it go with Korby?"

He smiled, Benedict Cumberbatch in a National Theatre revival of *The School for Scandal* that has all London agog. "What a sweetheart. Right? We've talked of moving in together, only his place is too small."

Following him to the door, I said, "You're going to give up that monster sublet of yours?"

"Everything's curable when you're in a hit," he replied, which didn't answer my question. "Next stop, one of those unbearably prestigious cable series."

He shook my hand, winked his all-bigged-up-now wink, and left.

I'll wrap this up symmetrically, on another weekend picnic in the park with Ken and Davey-Boy. Cosgrove had packed a basket for us—an actual wicker basket with interior leather straps to anchor the various containers, which I had no idea we owned. And, bless his heart, he had made hundred-taste meat loaf sandwiches. With cucumber salad and individual crocs of Santiago relish.

And of course Ken had smuggled in one of Tom-Tom's jars of French jam, for which I have acquired a taste.

"What was that song your buddy was singing?" Davey-Boy asked me, as we took in the passing gentry. "'Will Jizz For Pie?'"

"'If I Knew You Were Comin' I'd've Baked a Cake.'"

"Tom-Tom says there's a brand of this," said Ken, of the jam, "where they make it without sugar."

"Alert to shirtless very older bald guy crossing the road from the baseball diamonds," said Davey-Boy. "Totally build."

We looked: at a possible fifty-something in jeans and sandals, the beltline unfastened for maximum impression. Not so tall, but with a walk of great authority. His hair, around his skull and dusting his forehead, was grey. So was his bushy mustache and so were his eyes, in a match so incandescent that we could make them out at twenty yards. Further, he was in implausibly good shape, the torso rising in a grandiose V to a heavy chest and water-polo shoulders.

"Heading right for us," Davey-Boy noted.

"He's angry," said Ken.

I asked, "Can I have some more of that jam?"

Ken passed the jar over as Davey-Boy let out a low whistle.

"Look who's with him," he said—and I suddenly knew who was with him without looking.

It was Alex. And that must be Neil. But this improv wasn't going so well, because Alex seemed to be hanging back with a morose look. He'll spot me any moment, I thought—but he was too absorbed in the scene, fixed on his costar. Neil had crossed the road; pointing at Alex, he then pointed at the ground with a "Right here and I mean now!" attitude. Alex shook his head even as he slowly went up to Neil.

"'Come to Daddy,'" said Davey-Boy, creating the soundtrack, as he likes to do.

"You know that guy?" Ken asked.

"'Why be you so headstrong?'" Davey-Boy went on. "'You know my ways to make a handsome fella pay me mind.'"

"Don't swipe all the jam," Ken warned me as Alex wove his way through bikers and strollers to come up to Neil.

"'You'll take it fresh from the cock,'" Davey-Boy went on, riffing on what Alex had said in the improv class. "'You'll scarf up every drop, or I'll find out why but good.'"

Alex started to say something to Neil, but he gave up with a hopeless look as Neil laid a hand on the back of Alex's neck and slowly propelled him northward along the path, away from us.

I said, "Alex told me he was giving that whole scene up." Didn't he?

"'Giving me up?'" Davey-Boy echoed. "'When I

get you home, you'll turn over like a flapjack in a shantytown hash house.'"

I'd never heard anything quite that spicy from Davey-Boy before, and as I turned to him to comment, Ken took the jam from me.

"Hey!"

"You weren't sharing properly, cousin," said Ken. "Aren't you going to say hello to your friend?"

"They were right in front of us," I noted. "Inches off, really. If Alex had looked this way—"

"Actors don't do any looking," Davey-Boy observed. "Actors are looked at."

"Scope the crowd staring at them, will you? Haven't they ever seen a sex monster dragging his unwilling boy friend home for crashbang sex before?"

Ken giggled.

"'Come along, lad,'" Davey-Boy continued, as Neil and Alex went on up the road. "'If you're an actor, then you can act the way I say to, and show respect with expert cocksucking such as you actors know how to do. Then I'll ball you roughways but, after, I'll hold you in my arms, to make you as tenderhearted as can be. Because daddy knows best.'"

"I don't notice *you* sharing that jam all of a sudden."

"Too much jam is no good for a writer. It'll make you drowsy."

"Look how daddy still has his hands on the actor's neck," said Davey-Boy. "So dangerous and protective." After a moment, he added, "Ekcetera."

Ken handed me the jam, and as I spooned up the last morsels, Ken said, "Didn't you say that actor guy had destiny control now, with a hit play and any boy friend he chooses?" Watching me finish off the jam as though he'd suffered sharer's remorse and was going to snatch the jar back, he added, "Not a care in the world, you said."

"Yes, well, you can *play* the Heavy Father. But you can't be one unless you are one." Sucking on the very last spoonful, I went on, "It's a problem for actors, because all the gay world's a stage, and if you play on it long enough you don't really know who you are any more. It becomes…well…it becomes one endless puppet show."

"What are you," Ken asked, taking the jam jar to peer inside it, "the Hungry Tiger of Oz?"

Davey-Boy said, "He's the wicked storyteller of Manhattan, where all his friends fall victim to love racketeers."

That got him a look from Ken, and I said, "Don't blame me, boys," as I got out my little Staples notepad and a Pilot rolling ball black pen, extra fine. "I'm only the messenger."

ACKNOWLEDGMENTS

To my agent, Joe Spieler; to Clint Bocock and Michael Scalisi; and to my publisher, Don Weise.

ABOUT THE AUTHOR

Ethan Mordden's work has appeared in *The New Yorker* (three short stories, A Critic At Large features, and book review leads), the *New York Times*, and the *Wall Street Journal*. His *Christopher Street* column, *Is There a Book In This*? gave birth to the five volumes of gay stories known as the Buddies series, about a "family" of friends enjoying life and love in Manhattan. Mordden's non-fiction includes books on New York cultural history (The *Guest List: How Manhattan Defined American Sophistication*), opera, Hollywood, and Broadway, including a six-volume history of the American musical. He lives in New York.

CPSIA information can be obtained at www.ICGtesting.com
Printed in the USA
LVOW07s1555191015

458850LV00001B/21/P